eam.
"

But her words had no effect on him whatsoever. The nearer Saskia got, the more of Connor she could see, and the clearer it became that he was definitely not awake. Perspiration glistened against the muscles of his bare, smooth chest. His bedclothes were flung every which way, with only a red sheet wrapping him at the waist, dipping lower and lower as he tossed and turned.

Her mouth went dry. The man was gorgeous. The man was half-naked. Blood pounded in her veins, and her hands ached to touch him. It wasn't fair to stand there and stare at him when he was suffering from a nightmare, but what could she do?

Her mind went wild with the possibilities. Trying to remember to breathe, she set an unsteady hand on his hard forearm, sizzling her fingers where she touched him.

"Darling, is that you?" he asked fuzzily.

"Darling? Uh, no. No, I don't think so," Saskia tried, but it was too late. Connor's strong arm snaked out and reeled her in. Before she knew what hit her, she was wedged underneath him, trapped by his body in that big, soft bed.

ABOUT THE AUTHOR

Julie Kistler has always been fascinated by ghosts
and spirits and things that go bump in the night.
Dream Lover is her attempt to combine her usual
warped sense of humor with a lot of romance, a few love
potions and a crazy witch or two. She also added a cat
in honor of her own cat, Thisbe. Julie lives a sedentary
life in central Illinois with her tall, dark and handsome
husband.

Books by Julie Kistler

HARLEQUIN AMERICAN ROMANCE

JULIE KISTLER

DREAM LOVER

Harlequin Books

TORONTO • NEW YORK • LONDON
AMSTERDAM • PARIS • SYDNEY • HAMBURG
STOCKHOLM • ATHENS • TOKYO • MILAN
MADRID • WARSAW • BUDAPEST • AUCKLAND

TRUELOVE FAMILY TREE

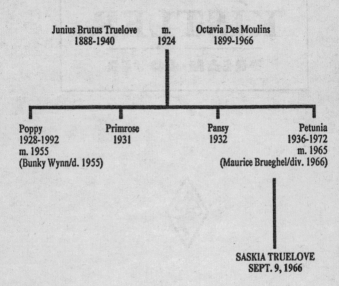

Junius Brutus Truelove   m.   Octavia Des Moulins
1888-1940   1924   1899-1966

Poppy
1928-1992
m. 1955
(Bunky Wynn/d. 1955)

Primrose
1931

Pansy
1932

Petunia
1936-1972
m. 1965
(Maurice Brueghel/div. 1966)

SASKIA TRUELOVE
SEPT. 9, 1966

WYNN FAMILY TREE

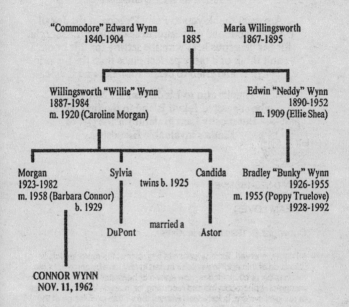

"Commodore" Edward Wynn
1840-1904

m.
1885

Maria Willingsworth
1867-1895

Willingsworth "Willie" Wynn
1887-1984
m. 1920 (Caroline Morgan)

Edwin "Neddy" Wynn
1890-1952
m. 1909 (Ellie Shea)

Morgan
1923-1982
m. 1958 (Barbara Connor)
b. 1929

Sylvia

twins b. 1925

Candida

Bradley "Bunky" Wynn
1926-1955
m. 1955 (Poppy Truelove)
1928-1992

DuPont

married a

Astor

CONNOR WYNN
NOV. 11, 1962

ACKNOWLEDGMENT

A special thank-you to Patty Durden at the Jekyll
Island Club Hotel on beautiful Jekyll Island, Georgia,
for her generous help with the setting for this book. I
can't think of a more perfect place than the historic
Jekyll Island Club to create romance and magic.

Thanks also to Linda Jenkins Nutting,
who suggested Jekyll Island in the first place.
But mostly I am grateful for the gift of
Linda's invaluable friendship.

ISBN 0-373-16535-8

DREAM LOVER

Chapter One

The wind howled and the rain pounded. A loose shutter slapped against the outside of the house somewhere, banging out an irregular, uneasy rhythm.

Saskia shivered. She switched on yet another lamp in the parlor, but it didn't help. It was already downright spooky around here, and the séance hadn't even begun.

"I think we may be having a hurricane," she said uneasily, as she peered out the french doors into the storm. But all she could see was a gray wall of rain, slashing almost sideways as it beat on the glass.

What made it even more frightening was that she had never lived on the coast before, she didn't know what precautions she ought to be taking. Saskia wished, not for the first time, that the house were more secure.

She wasn't at all sure the roof wouldn't fly right off, or the walls cave in, or the newly repaired north tower tumble to the ground under this kind on onslaught. Her renovation plans had yielded plenty of bills, all piled neatly on the rolltop desk in the library, and she didn't need any more, storm or no storm.

She also wished she had a television. Tuning in to some nice steady anchorperson would've been lovely at the moment, and she made a mental note to find a TV the next time she was off the island. Right now, all she had to look at was that dark, brooding portrait of Commodore Wynn, the original owner of the house. He wasn't offering any useful information. All he ever did was glower at her.

She really ought to get rid of that painting. There was something very disturbing about it and the man in it. Saskia wondered idly if it was worth anything. She'd have to make a note to take it to some kind of art appraiser.

"A hurricane! How exciting!" Aunt Petunia exclaimed, turning from her incense burner, clapping her plump hands together. "A hurricane is the perfect setting to call forth spirits. So electrifying! So elemental! Don't you think so, Primrose?"

Petunia's sister Primrose, older by ten months, seemed less enthusiastic. "Will the spirits travel through the rain?" she asked anxiously. "Perhaps they don't like to get wet."

"I don't think spirits get wet, darling." Trying not to choke on the heavy, sweet smell of the jasmine incense, Saskia found a smile for Primrose. "I'm not so sure about Madame Renata, though. She's coming from Jacksonville, right? Is she driving up, do you think?"

Petunia tipped her pale violet-tinted curls to one side. "How else would she get here? She wouldn't come by boat in this sort of weather, surely."

Saskia had been thinking more on the order of a broom, but she held her tongue. She had never met her aunts' newest friend, a highly suspicious woman who billed herself as a trance medium, willing and able to conjure up the dear departed at the drop of a hat. Petunia and Primrose had discovered the woman at a psychic fair, and they were simply sure she was the genuine article.

She's exactly what we need to finally make a connection to the spirit world, the aunts kept repeating. Saskia wasn't so sure.

Especially with the wind and the rain and all the other portents of disaster. Outside, the thunder boomed even louder, sending shivers of fear up her spine, and she regretted the whole scheme. She would never have agreed to the séance if she really believed Madame Renata had any unearthly powers. No, she just wanted to see the process firsthand, to take some notes, perhaps pick up a few hints for later use.

Once Wynnwood was completely refurbished in all its glory, turned into a comfy if eccentric bed-and-breakfast, Saskia planned to offer mystery and ghost-hunting weekend packages. The house had the perfect reputation—chock-full of stories about haunted rooms and family curses—and Saskia had decided that séances in the parlor would be the perfect touch.

But there was no way she'd be able to afford a professional medium, especially after all those repair bills drained her bank account. Making Wynnwood into something special had already cost an arm and a leg.

Besides, how difficult could it be to spout some spooky-sounding words and pretend to talk to a few ghosts? Surely she could watch a real medium in action and fake it herself the next time, or maybe even convince one of her aunts to do it. Petunia and Primrose loved anything to do with the occult, so it shouldn't be that big a leap to convince them to conduct séances.

But now that she'd had a chance to think it over, Saskia wasn't at all sure *tonight* was the best choice to get started. The crash of thunder and lightning, the roar of wind and rain... If Wynnwood really did have ghosts, this was the perfect night for them to start crawling out of the woodwork.

As if to confirm her thoughts, the wind took up a particularly horrifying howl. Banquo, her aunts' big black cat, meowed loudly, staring out through the cold glass of the french doors, as if he, too, expected some sort of phantom to come lurching in at any moment.

"Banquo, get away from there," Saskia muttered, shooing at the cat and forcing herself to turn away from the door. But that brought her face-to-face with that gloomy portrait, glaring at her from over the fireplace. Was it her imagination, or had the Commodore's painted expression gotten even more forbidding? She shivered again.

"Maybe Madame Renata won't be able to get here tonight," she said hopefully.

"Not get here?" Aunt Primrose echoed. "Oh, dear, no! The candles, the incense, the little cakes—everything is ready. This is the perfect night, Saskia. We must do it tonight, or wait until..." Her brow furrowed with concentration. "Oh, dear, I've forgotten the next possible date. Full moon, planets in alignment... I'll have to do the charts," she murmured. "Of course, I already did them once, and I might be better off locating the first go-round. Tempting fate, you know, to—"

But a vigorous pounding at the front door drowned out Primrose's words, cutting through even the noise of the storm. "That must be her!" Aunt Petunia announced as she scampered out into the hallway.

Saskia followed, feeling a bit apprehensive about what might lie on the other side of the front door. Weren't mediums supposed to be ethereal, delicate people? That sounded more like the meaty fist of a lumberjack.

Saskia slipped into the vestibule behind Petunia just as the door swung open, slashing wind and rain into the front hall, almost knocking tiny Petunia over completely.

And in blew Madame Renata.

"Greetings!" she announced in a very theatrical voice, tossing off a huge rain-spattered cape, revealing a gauzy purple dress with silver stars and moons scattered over it. "Madame Renata has arrived."

"Thank goodness you're here. We were worried," Aunt Primrose told her.

But Madame Renata just waved one hand, as if dismissing the idea that mere weather could stop her. Bending to retrieve the discarded cape, Saskia had a chance to take in the whole picture from the bottom up. It was pretty impressive, she had to admit.

Madame Renata was a large woman, big-boned and tall, although it was impossible to tell exactly what she was hiding under the expansive folds of her gauzy violet dress, with its bat-wing sleeves and flowing lines. She was wearing a turban made up in the same glittery fabric, with a big silver pin in the shape of a star clasped to the front. Every finger held a silver ring or two, all winking with violet and blue stones. Very cosmic. Very impressive.

Saskia tried to put the best face on things. Even though this was all so unusual, it was no time to forget her manners. "I'm Saskia Truelove." She smiled and held out a hand. "I've heard a lot about you from my aunts."

But the medium ignored her. Without a word, Renata strode right past Saskia and her outstretched hand, trooping down the hall and into the parlor, leaving the others to simply trail along in her wake. Saskia had a moment to doubt when she realized that Madame Renata had headed directly for the parlor without asking for directions. She'd never been to Wynnwood before. So how did she know where to go?

Maybe the medium really *was* psychic.

"Don't be absurd," Saskia murmured, getting a sudden inspiration. "It's the incense, of course. She just followed her nose."

As Renata strode into the parlor, casting an imperious eye over the round wooden table and four chairs set up in the center of the room, studying the precise arrangement of candles, Petunia and Primrose fluttered nervously behind her.

"Is it too dark?" Primrose asked, gazing around at the assortment of flickering lights.

"Or too light?" Petunia tried. She switched off the small, fringed lamp on the mantel, the one Saskia had lit not ten minutes ago. "We want everything to be perfect for you, Madame Renata."

"Perfect," her sister chorused, turning the same light back on.

"Silence!" Madame Renata commanded. "I am absorbing the psychic vibrations."

"Oh, absorbing. Isn't that interesting?" Petunia murmured.

"Very interesting," Primrose agreed.

"Silence!"

This time the sisters managed to hold onto their simmering excitement, but their wide eyes followed the medium's every move. Madame Renata stalked around the small parlor, sniffing at the incense, squinting at the cake plate full of pretty little petits fours. She closed her eyes momentarily and swayed just a bit to one side, then abruptly righted herself and flung herself down into a heavy armchair they'd set at the head of the table.

"A glass of red wine. Here!" she ordered, slapping a hand on the edge of the table.

"Oh, dear." Primrose gave her niece a mournful look. "I don't think we have any wine."

"Of course we do, darling," Saskia said quickly, moving to the sideboard and pulling out a cut-glass decanter of dreadful elderberry wine that she knew her aunts liked to nip into when she wasn't around. She found a glass and filled it right to the rim for the medium. "Spirits for the spirits," she said gaily.

Renata frowned, clearly not appreciating the joke. Neither did whoever was outside orchestrating the storm. Thunder crashed and lightning sizzled just as Saskia set down the glass. She jumped, almost spilling the wine, sending a startled glance at the medium. Did she do that?

"The spirits are restless," Madame Renata intoned. "We must begin."

"Oh, yes, yes, by all means," the aunts whispered together.

"But first, I will need a small comestible, something to energize me and enable my trance."

"A comestible?" Primrose asked doubtfully.

"Something to eat," Saskia told her. "I think she means those tea cakes she told you to make."

"Oh, yes." Petunia hurried to move the plate closer to the medium's greedy hand.

As she ate three little frosted white cakes in one gulp, Madame Renata spat out instructions with the crumbs. "The spirits require three candles, white ones, placed in a triangle in the center of the table. Otherwise, darkness." She pointed a long finger at each of them in turn. "Then you must sit, you ladies directly across from each other, and you," she said to Saskia, "across from me. Please leave equal spaces in between. The candles must form a triangle inside the circle of the table, inside the square of our beings."

The three members of her audience exchanged confused glances.

"The triangle inside the circle inside the square," Renata repeated impatiently. "And then you will remain perfectly silent and still, while I enter my trance state. Once my spirit guide has arrived, he may pose questions to better direct your inquiry. Please answer him, but do not ask questions of your own. The spirits do not appreciate being cross-examined."

Saskia frowned, hanging back from the table. She had never had the slightest inkling that she was psychic herself, but she was getting some very bad vibes about tonight's little soirée. Her aunts were eating this up, positively quivering with glee, while the unhappy medium was behaving like a real pain in the neck.

Meanwhile, Petunia moved three white candles, as instructed, and Primrose turned off all the other lights. They took the seats next to Madame Renata, motioning Saskia to join them at the table.

"Maybe I should—"

"Sit!" Renata boomed, and Saskia leapt into her chair. "I am ready to begin. Hands, please." The medium grabbed for Petunia's plump little hand on her right and Primrose's bonier fingers on her left. "Now concentrate. Focus on the image of the loved one you seek to contact. Keep that image constant."

Saskia pretended to oblige, taking one each of her aunts' hands. Under the table, she could feel Banquo winding himself around her legs, purring and rubbing loudly, adding his own sleek electricity to the proceedings. She was going to start giving off sparks soon, what with the cat's static and the tension from the storm.

She knew very well whom her aunts wanted to reach, but she had no intention of cooperating or conjuring up mental pictures of poor Aunt Poppy. The eldest of the Truelove sisters, Poppy had been dead almost a year now—rest in peace—and Saskia fully expected her to stay that way.

After all, Poppy had lived a long and happy life right here at Wynnwood. Saskia frowned. Well, it hadn't been all that happy, actually.

The Truelove women were not known for stable relationships, regardless of the cozy sentiment of their last name. In fact, when it came to matters of the heart, they were downright disasters. Saskia's own mother, Pansy, the youngest of the Truelove sisters, had been married for a total of eighteen months, and she'd had the best love life of the bunch.

At first, Aunt Poppy's life had seemed to be breaking the mold of the Truelove predilection for unhappy endings. Just like any normal woman, she'd fallen in love and gotten married. As a matter of fact, Poppy Truelove had come to Wynnwood as a bride.

Unfortunately, she'd immediately lost the groom to a wayward birdbath. One conk on the head, and Poppy's new husband was no more.

All Poppy got out of the deal was Wynnwood, a Gothic monstrosity of a house. She'd spent the forty years after her husband's untimely passing wandering around the hideous old house, selling off artifacts and furnishings as necessary to pay the bills, and all the while hosting every kind of séance and spiritualist gathering around, trying to reestablish contact with her poor dead groom. Of course, she'd never heard a peep.

But now that Poppy was gone, her surviving sisters were determined to pick up where she'd left off in the séance department. They'd taken up residence in Wynnwood like their sister before them, and now they thought they had a medium who would patch them through to the Great Beyond.

Was Poppy happy out there somewhere? Had she finally been reunited with Bunky Wynn, the love of her life? The Truelove sisters were burning with questions for their departed sibling, and nothing, not even a hurricane, was going to stop them.

Saskia gazed fondly at her sweet, deluded aunts. Petunia was positively beaming, drinking in the experience of the séance, while Primrose, always a less enthusiastic soul, squeezed her eyes shut. Saskia compromised by half closing her eyes, wishing she had never let them start this nonsense.

It was scary enough living in eerie old Wynnwood, with its creaky staircases and winding passageways. If there was a square room in the house, she hadn't found it yet. Everything was slightly off center, off kilter, a little weird.

Life at Wynnwood was perfect for black cats and poltergeists, but somewhat stressful for a normal person such as Saskia. Of course, with her upbringing, she'd had very few opportunities to know what normal was, but she knew *this* wasn't it.

But there was no tie for speculation at the moment. As her aunts tightened their grips on either side of her, Saskia kept an eye on Madame Renata. She appeared to be dozing, eyes closed, with her chin pressed into her chest. She was mumbling some sort of incantation, but so softly that it was impossible to discern any actual words or syllables.

"I call upon you, Mike," she said suddenly, in a chesty, rumbling voice. "Mike, come to me."

"Mike?" Saskia asked doubtfully. "Who's Mike?"

"Her spirit guide," Petunia whispered.

"What kind of name is Mike for a spirit?"

Madame Renata's eyes popped open and she glared at Saskia. "You don't get to choose your spirit guide. You take who you get."

"Oh. Sorry."

"Will you please be quiet so I can get through? Your incessant chatter is clogging up my transmission." She closed her eyes again and commanded, "Now focus on the one you seek. I will try to make contact through Mike."

Dutifully, Saskia kept her mouth shut, as her brain went wild with visions of harried telephone operators sitting on a cloud somewhere, connecting and disconnecting spirit calls. *I'm sorry, that line is busy. Would you like to try redialing?*

"Mike, are you there?" the medium called out, and then she answered herself, whispering, "Yes, Renata, I have arrived to guide you," in a high-pitched, tinny voice that sounded like no Mike Saskia had ever met.

"Oh, my word!" Petunia murmured, her eyes as round as saucers. "That does sound like a spirit, doesn't it?"

Only if the spirit has been inhaling helium, Saskia thought unkindly.

Renata's head dropped back and her mouth fell open. "I have journeyed a long way to come to you tonight," she said, in that same thin, quavery voice. "Through wind and rain and storm, through many lives and many ages."

Well, that was a good line, with lots of atmosphere. She'd have to remember that one.

"I feel the spirits all around me," Mike continued. "They are very agitated here in this place. This is a place of old unhappiness, of lives entwined and knotted, souls still seeking earthly peace and celestial reward. Many voices."

"That's what Poppy always said," Petunia whispered loudly. "That this house was full of unhappy souls. Do you see a curse?" she asked hopefully. "Poppy thought there was a curse, left by Commodore Wynn, the first owner of the house. Plus, of course, this Truelove curse. We all know about that, don't we, girls?"

"A curse... Possibly a curse. So many spirits. It's hard to tell..."

"I want to talk to Poppy!" Primrose interrupted. Speaking to the air somewhere over the medium's head, she called out, "Sister, dear, are you there?"

"Please," Madame Renata implored, still in her helium-inspired "Mike" voice, "you must refrain from shouting. You appeal to the spirit of your sister, Poppy, is that correct? Your sister has recently passed to the other side, and you seek some word?"

"Exactly." Petunia squeezed Saskia's hand. "This 'Mike' spirit sees everything so clearly. Isn't it exciting?"

"I seek Poppy," the spirit moaned. "But what I see is the shadow of unhappiness. Death. Sadness. Hearts divided." She peeked out from under one eyelid. "A broken heart, perhaps?"

"Oh, yes!" Primrose nodded emphatically. "That would definitely be Poppy. She was married in this house, you know. And then the poor man died on their honeymoon, right here. Knocked his head on a birdbath and that was that."

"I see it, yes," "Mike" responded, once more picking up the cues the aunts dropped. "A young man, so very handsome, so full of love. And his bride, a lovely young flower of a woman. She's breathtaking in her white dress."

White dress? Saskia pressed her lips together, keeping her mouth shut even if it killed her. There was a wedding photo of Poppy and Bunky Wynn at the top of the stairs. Poppy had worn a bright red suit to get married in. The color of poppies, of course.

"I see many flowers," the medium continued. "The garden. Did he die in the garden?"

"Yes, he did," Petunia buzzed, bobbing in her chair and wiggling Saskia's left hand. "That's exactly right! Isn't that simply amazing?"

"Hmm," Saskia murmured. Primrose had let it slip that Bunky died when he hit his head on a birdbath. And where else would a birdbath be if not in the garden?

So far, "Mike" had spoken in a funny voice and parroted back the same information the aunts had given him. Not exactly supernatural.

"The beautiful young man... His name was... It's very unclear, but I think I see an A..."

"No, no, that's not him," Primrose prompted. "Try again."

"B...?" the spirit tried, going alphabetically.

Saskia really didn't think it was fair that Bunky's name had popped up right at the beginning of the alphabet, completely by accident, but once again her aunts were impressed with the medium's "power" and "insight."

Petunia was ready to burst with excitement. "Yes, that's it. I can't believe it! B for Bunky. Bunky Wynn."

But the medium was already sailing away on her spiritual sea. "I see much sorrow, much grieving," she said loudly. "Oh, he died, didn't he? How sad." Her voice drifted away slowly. "And his young bride was left behind, in this house, never to forget him, always remembering. Is that right?"

"Oh, yes. That's right."

The aunts were vying to see who could tell the story first. Petunia won, as usual.

"Bunky and Poppy were so in love, but they were only married for two weeks. He was one of the hoity-toity Wynns, you know, a direct descendant of Commodore Wynn, who built the house. The one in the portrait. A dreadful man. Very cold and unfeeling. That's what Poppy said. He didn't approve of that side of the family and cut them off without a dime. All Bunky got was this house."

"Ah, yes. The house. Poppy's voice comes to me, over the years. I hear Poppy saying, 'My beloved

Bunky, where are you? Why have you left me behind?' ''

"Oh, that is *so* true. Why, she said that all the time, didn't she?"

"Always," Primrose confirmed.

"Is Poppy there?" Petunia asked eagerly. "Can we speak to Poppy?"

Renata's voice became much fainter when she said, "She is with Bunky at last. She says to tell you she is very happy, very joyful. Poppy, come closer—your sisters wish to speak to you. Come to us, Poppy. Come to us now..."

"Oh, yes, please!" Primrose cried.

"Poppy, dear, please speak to us. We have missed you dreadfully," Petunia added.

She can't hear you, darling, Saskia wanted to say. She held her tongue only with extreme self-control.

She didn't mind a bit of fun, but this was going too far. If Madame Renata was planning for one minute to impersonate Aunt Poppy, dragging all their emotions through the wringer, taking advantage of two dear, sweet old ladies... Well, Saskia was not going to sit still for *that*.

"Poppy's presence is becoming stronger. I feel her..." the spirit guide whispered. "She's going to speak now..."

"Oh, no, she's not," Saskia said grimly. "This has gone far enough—"

"Quiet!" Renata growled, losing most of her high, spooky voice as she rose from her seat. "The spirits do not like your insolence. Your disbelief has made them very angry!"

The words were no sooner out of her mouth than the whole house began to shake. Saskia stood, horrified, as the windowpanes rattled, as the charged air seethed around her, as that nasty portrait of Commodore Wynn bumped against the wall and slipped to one side. An unearthly roar filled her ears as the candles on the table flickered wildly.

Was this a hurricane? Or the combined wrath of a houseful of ghosts?

Saskia had no time to wonder. A jagged bolt of lightning flashed outside the french doors and a fierce peal of thunder boomed so loud and so close that it reverberated around the parlor.

"Spirits, we welcome you!" Renata shouted, but it was hard to hear her over the storm. "Spirits, heed my words! Arise and make yourselves known to us!"

With a fearsome whoosh, the french doors blew open and cold, hard, furious rain poured into the parlor, dousing the candles, slashing the room with shadows. The cat let out a yowl and streaked past Saskia's leg.

Lightning blazed again, illuminating the room for just a second. And then total darkness consumed them.

"What the hell is going on here?" a man's voice demanded.

A man? Saskia's heart leapt to her throat. *Whose voice was that?*

Suddenly, the small lamp over the fireplace flashed on. A tall, handsome, extremely angry man stood next to it. He was glaring at all of them, but they just stood there, frozen in their places.

Until Aunt Petunia recovered her voice. "Oh, my word! It's Commodore Wynn!" she cried, pointing at the painting that hung over his left shoulder.

Behind her, Madame Renata gave out a shriek that really would've raised the dead. Saskia's eyes shot from the portrait to the man who was standing in front of it.

"Oh, my God," she said out loud.

Petunia was right. It was the Commodore.

Chapter Two

At the moment, he was very annoyed and very wet. He did not appreciate either condition.

At first, there was complete silence, while everybody stared at him with their mouths hanging open.

Then a large woman in a very strange outfit suddenly howled, "Oh, my God! I really did it!" She closed her eyes, made a sort of a "wmph" noise, and crumpled into a heap on the rug. The crazy turban thing she was wearing fell off and rolled under the table.

"Oh, dear! Oh, my!" somebody shrieked. Or maybe more than one somebody. It was hard to tell, with everybody jumping around.

A pretty brunette who looked oddly familiar—did he know her?—rushed to help the woman who'd fainted, while two other older ladies fluttered and hovered, waving their hands, muttering and mumbling, practically spinning with nerves and adrenaline.

Everyone seemed to be sputtering at once, and he couldn't make heads or tails of what was going on.

Some sort of incense was burning in the parlor, sending thin tendrils of sweet smoke into the air, and he sneezed twice as he tried to figure out where it was coming from so he could get away from it.

"It sneezed!" one old lady exclaimed, hopping as she hugged the other one's arm. "I didn't know spirits could sneeze, did you, sister?"

What had she just called him? He must've misheard, what with the jumble of noise coming from the storm and the chattering old ladies. He shook his head, trying not to breathe that sickly sweet smoke. All those candles, and incense, too... Taking up residence in a house they didn't own was one thing, but trying to burn the place down was quite another.

"What's going on here?" he demanded, shouting to be heard over the roar of thunder and wind.

"It speaks!" the old lady shrieked. "Oh, my goodness! How exciting!"

"Oh, dear, oh, dear," the other one whimpered. "I told you not to use jasmine. Now look what you've done!"

The first one declared, "It was supposed to help us reach the spirits. And it's worked perfectly, hasn't it?" And then she advanced on him, reaching up and pinching him hard on the arm. "Solid as a rock," she concluded. "A complete physical manifestation. Isn't it remarkable?"

He backed away quickly, getting his arm out of range of her poking fingers. Retreat seemed to be his only defense at the moment. He could hardly knock away an old lady, even if she was loose a few screws.

Meanwhile, the rain was still pouring in the open french doors, and it appeared he was the only one with enough sense to close them. As they continued to stare at him, all aquiver, he quickly slammed the doors shut. The large woman on the floor began to stir, mumbling and moaning. The brunette at her side hoisted her to a sitting position, fanning her florid face. "Are you all right?" she asked anxiously.

The woman mumbled something, but the brunette took time out from her ministrations to look up and sizzle him with an angry glare. "How dare you come in here, pretending to be the Commodore and scaring everyone?"

"I didn't pretend to be anything," he shot back. He wanted to defend himself, but he was too distracted by that same sharp, heady feeling that he *knew* her. But surely he'd remember if they'd met before.

"You're certainly not Commodore Wynn," she returned. "The man's been dead for seventy years."

"But he most definitely *is* him," the pinching lady argued. "Or at least the spiritual manifestation. Why, he looks just like him."

"Spiritual manifestation? What does that mean?" But suddenly all the mumbo jumbo fell into place. They thought he was a ghost. The ghost of Commodore Wynn. "Me? You've got to be kidding!"

He spared a glance for the portrait they were all comparing him to. He realized there was a certain superficial resemblance there—the same color or hair and eyes, maybe even the same square jaw—but that was it. And he didn't have that surly sneer, either. No, he was clearly no commodore, even if he allowed for the fact that they were crazy enough to believe in ghosts in the first place.

Anyone with a thimbleful of sense would've taken one look at him—at this wet, cranky man, just barely hanging onto the last shreds of his temper after being rained on, pinched, shouted at and generally mistreated—and known without a doubt how human and real he was.

He flung out one arm of his dark trench coat, spraying water all over the rug. Darkly, he asked, "Do ghosts drip on the carpet?"

"It's very clear what happened," the old lady persisted. "We were conjuring up spirits, trying to get Poppy, but the Commodore manifested by mistake. Just like dialing a wrong number. I'm sure Madame Renata will tell us that this sort of thing happens all the time."

"I don't think she's saying anything at the moment, Aunt Petunia," the brunette noted tactfully.

So Aunt Petunia was the purple-haired pincher, and Madame Renata was the name of the semiconscious one in the jazzy getup. He shook his head, still not believing what he'd walked into. "So you were all sitting around conjuring up ghosts, and she was your channeler?"

"I prefer to be called a medium," the lady in question said grandly, as she heaved herself to her hands and knees and hunted around for her turban. "Channelers are nothing more than a bunch of New Age nonsense. *I'm* a traditionalist."

It was all nonsense as far as he was concerned.

The self-proclaimed medium crammed her turban back on her head and sat down at the table, reaching for her wineglass. "I find myself in dire need of refreshment." She poured it full and then knocked back most of it in one swallow.

"Fine," he muttered. "As for the rest of you, you're all Trueloves, aren't you?"

"He knows our names!" Petunia said happily, clapping her hands together.

"I know more than that." He reached into his side pocket, retrieving a damp brochure. He shook it out. "I know that a bunch of you have set up camp here, trading on the Wynn family history. I know you're pretending the place is haunted, and you're running some kind of con game for tourists."

"Con game?" the one who was not Petunia gasped. "You're not running a con game, are you, Saskia?"

The old lady's words faded out as he looked deep into the eyes of the beautiful young woman in front of him. *Saskia.* That was the name on the brochure, and that was what the old lady had called her. *Saskia Truelove.*

Of course.

He might've expected her to be some sort of outlandish, bizarre character, someone more like the tipsy medium in the turban, still chugging down wine at her séance table. But Saskia was nothing like that old fraud. No, she was very real. And very beautiful.

She was also very, very familiar. In a way he couldn't shake, even if he didn't understand it.

He could swear he'd never seen her before, but somehow she set off a whole chorus of bells clanging deep inside him. Was this recognition, or maybe just a warning?

She had soft brown hair, worn full and loose around her face, and wide, deep brown eyes. Right now those eyes were sparkling with spirit, intelligence, outrage and an excess of exhilaration, as if the storm and the electricity in the room were pulsing through her. He felt it, too.

Her features—so achingly, tantalizingly familiar—drew his eyes. Thoughtfully, irresistibly, he let his gaze trace the fullness of her bottom lip, the stubborn line of her jaw, the warm, rosy glow of her cheeks.

So this was Saskia Truelove, his adversary.

Even though it had only been five minutes since he'd first laid eyes on her, something inside him told him he understood her through and through. Instinctively, he knew that she had the habit of lifting one eyebrow when she was bemused, that her skin was softer than rose petals, that her chin rose stubbornly when she was backed into a corner.

And he knew exactly how to manipulate her. Right out of his house, if that's what he wanted.

That *was* what he wanted, wasn't it?

Well, it had been until five minutes ago. One good look at her and he suddenly had the bizarre feeling that the two of them had been fighting the same battle of wills for centuries. And no matter how many times he won that battle, he'd always lose the war.

"Bizarre," he muttered. He shook his head, trying to dispel these odd, woozy thoughts.

It was late; he was tired. That was all there was to it. He didn't really recognize her or know her, and whatever inside information his brain was sending him was based on the fact that he was a good judge of character and a very crafty businessman. Nothing more.

So why did he still feel so strange?

Saskia stared at him, puzzled, rapt, as if she, too, felt this curious tug of chemistry or déjà vu or whatever it was.

"Have we . . . ?" she began, but stopped before finishing the thought.

"What was he saying, Saskia?" the old lady asked querulously. "What did he mean?"

"It's all right, Aunt Primrose. We're not doing anything wrong. In fact," she said firmly, turning back to Connor, "there is nothing in the least improper about our plans for Wynnwood."

He managed a small smile. "And what about when I walked in?" He shook his head in Madame Renata's direction, making his opinion of such foolishness crystal clear. "Improper isn't the word for it."

Her color heightened. "There's nothing improper about a little séance. People have them every day." She frowned suddenly. "Why am I explaining this to you? It's no concern of yours what we do in the privacy of our own home."

"But, Saskia," the fussy sister, the one she'd called Primrose, began, "of course it's his concern. The Commodore built the house, after all. And now he doesn't want to have people running all around, disrupting the place where he's chosen to spend eternity. Isn't that right, Commodore?"

"I've been trying to tell you, I'm not the Commodore."

"Well then, who are you?" Saskia demanded. "So far, all we know is that you have a penchant for breaking and entering."

"Breaking and entering? When?"

"That's what it looks like to me," she said smartly, "when a person jimmies the lock and sashays into my parlor uninvited. So you'd better explain yourself pretty quick, mister, before I call the police on you."

"The police?" He smiled. It might create a few moments of discomfort, but he refused to take that kind of silliness seriously. He was a Wynn, for goodness' sake. He dismissed her threat with a wave of one aristocratic hand. "That would be a very bad move, Saskia. All you'd do is embarrass yourself."

"Oh, yeah?" She narrowed her eyes. "And why is that?"

"I'm Connor Wynn." He added softly, "The Commodore's great-grandson."

There was a long pause.

"The Commodore's great-grandson?" she echoed. "But . . . But what made you turn up *now?*"

"My timing may not be the best," he admitted, willing to be magnanimous. He had no intention of explaining why this errand had suddenly shot up to the top of his priority list. He wasn't sure he understood himself.

Under any stretch of the imagination, Wynnwood was of little importance to anyone in the family after all these years. Well, there were his mother and his grandmother, who both thought that it was disgraceful for a bunch of squatters to take up residence in a family home, no matter how remote, and then show every intention of swindling people into thinking it was a haunted house.

But that was hardly enough, under normal circumstances, to pry Connor out of his cushy office at the Wynn Building on Wall Street, sending him charging down to an island off the coast of Georgia just to play Big Bad Landlord.

Although he shared his mother and grandmother's dubious sentiments about exhuming the shadows of Wynns past, he could've just unleashed a fleet of lawyers on the Truelove women and forgotten about it.

But for whatever reason, he couldn't do that. He'd felt compelled to come down here and handle it himself.

This isn't like you, his mother had sniffed, and she was right.

But he hadn't been like himself, not since he'd been asked to put together a few photos and papers of the commodore for an exhibit at the new Wynn wing of the Metropolitan Museum, not since he'd started pawing around in his great-grandfather's papers, not since he'd run across that tantalizing reference to a series of statues called the Isabelle bronzes...

His great-grandfather had apparently paid a huge sum to a famous artist in 1904 for those bronzes, but they had never been seen among any of the Wynn collections. As nearly as Connor could tell, they had been left at Wynnwood all those years ago, before Bunky or Poppy or any of the other Trueloves showed up.

They could be junk, or they could be priceless. For that matter, they could be figments of some overzealous clerk's imagination. But he had been swept up by the feeling that he needed to find those statues, and every crumb of information he'd found had led him to believe they were still hidden somewhere at Wynnwood.

But he could hardly search the place if it was full of Trueloves and their ghost-busting guests. And so Connor could kill two birds with one stone, quite neatly, by dispossessing the old ladies first, and then conducting an organized, careful inventory of Wynnwood. That was the plan.

Until he met Saskia, and every hair on the back of his neck began to tingle with this uncanny precognition.

Now dispossession didn't seem like the best answer. But maybe a compromise of some sort...

"My timing isn't the best," he repeated, pulling himself away from any more of those mysterious vibrations about Saskia. "But it doesn't matter. I'm here now, and we have a problem."

"We do?" She crossed her arms over her chest. "Even if you are a Wynn, I don't see how that affects me."

"It affects your plan." He tapped her haunted-house brochure against the flat of his hand to remind her. Assuming a more normal Wynn family attitude, he said coolly, "You see, I can't allow you to turn this place into some sort of circus sideshow."

"Isn't that interesting, Primrose? The Commodore has got hold of one of Saskia's flyers in the spirit world." Aunt Petunia shook her lavender curls daintily. "I wasn't aware paper could penetrate the veil between this world and the next, were you, dear?"

"Connor Wynn, did he say?" her sister whispered loudly. "I don't recall any Connor among the family portraits, do you, Petunia? What era are you from, young man? Are you Edwardian? Or one of the Civil War Wynns?"

He declined to point out, once again, that he was from the *current* era. Whatever he said, it didn't seem to make any impression. He had almost forgotten the two elder Trueloves were there, until they made their usual dippy comments and exasperated him all over again. He couldn't recall ever being faced with a pair of dingdongs quite like these two, and he was at a loss how to deal with them.

"I do hope the house hasn't changed much since your time," Primrose continued with a look of distress. "I know our dear sister Poppy tried hard to keep everything just the way her darling Bunky left it. But I'm sure there will be many things that look strange to you—you know, indoor plumbing and such. And that must be so unsettling, to come back and find your house all disturbed and different."

"I'm glad you brought that up," Connor said quickly. He had no idea what she *had* brought up, but he wanted to make one important point on the double. "I'd like all of us to be clear on the fact that this really is *my* house."

"Well, of course it is, dear." Aunt Petunia patted his arm sweetly. "You built it, didn't you?"

"No, I didn't."

"He's not the Commodore, Aunt Petunia," Saskia tried from one side, but her words had as little effect as his, and Petunia swept on, blithely indifferent to them all.

"And then when you died," she said kindly, "you gave it to Bunky, didn't you? And Bunky left it to Poppy, and Poppy left it to us, and there you are. So you'll just have to get used to sharing it, won't you, dear?" she chattered. "Because after all, you're dead and we're not, so we get first dibs."

"He's not dead," Saskia protested, but Connor was willing to leave that alone for the moment.

"You have to understand that the house isn't yours," he tried. "And it wasn't Bunky's, either."

"Oh, pish posh! Of course it was Bunky's."

"But Bunky was the black sheep of the family," Connor explained. "He only lived here at the family's sufferance—they thought he was more likely to stay out of trouble if they banished him all the way down here. It didn't work, of course, because he married your sister."

"Are you suggesting that my Aunt Poppy was *trouble?*" Saskia demanded. "What exactly does that mean?"

"Well, that she wasn't the right sort of person . . ." He saw the look on her face, and he knew he was in deep water.

"You think because she was a Truelove, she wasn't good enough, is that it? Well, I'll have you know that Trueloves have been independent thinkers for generations." Her chin high, she told him, "We may not abide by the same idiotic rules and conventions as the rest of the sheep around us, but we bring creativity and passion to the world."

"Not to mention chaos," he mumbled.

It was generally accepted within the family that Bunky's long-ago marriage to "that scandalous Truelove woman" had been a disaster unprecedented in Wynn circles, for all the reasons Saskia had just enumerated. Like the rest of her family, Poppy had had no name, no money, no status, and from all accounts she was a raging flake. Her attempts to make hay off the Wynn name had been an embarrassment for all concerned.

But he could hardly say that to the woman's niece, could he?

"It doesn't matter," he said finally. "The important thing is that the house never belonged to Bunky."

"I really don't understand this," Saskia said with obvious spirit. "My Aunt Poppy lived in this house for almost forty years. If what you're saying is true, this wouldn't have been her house. Why weren't the mighty Wynns jumping in immediately to kick her out?"

Connor raked a hand through his soaked hair. Even though he felt absolutely sure that he was in the right, it was hard to destroy people's delusions when it came right down to it.

Awkwardly, he said, "As long as she was alive, the family thought it best to just leave her here. She was, after all, family of a sort, by virtue of marrying Bunky, and we could hardly turn her out. But now that she's gone ..."

"This can't be," Saskia murmured. "It simply can't be."

"Is that boy trying to suggest that we don't belong here?" Primrose asked anxiously.

"Don't worry," Petunia responded cheerfully. "Why, of course we belong here. Poppy left us everything, and this was Poppy's house. So now it's our house."

"But that's what I'm trying to tell you," he said patiently. "It wasn't—"

But Saskia grabbed his arm and dragged him over to the corner of the parlor, out of earshot of the others. "Please," she whispered, "I would prefer not to discuss this in front of my aunts. I don't want to upset them."

"But we really need to sort a few things out, as soon as possible. If you're going to cancel your ghost-busting weekends, you'll need to get the word out right away."

"Who says I'm going to cancel?"

"You don't have a choice."

She glanced back over at the old ladies, who were obviously trying to eavesdrop from a distance.

"They're going to have to hear the truth sooner or later," he told her.

"Then let's make it *later*," she said in a dark undertone. "Once I have it sorted out for myself, I can tell them whatever it is they need to know."

"I'm not sure I like the idea of prolonging this indefinitely."

"We're hardly going to jump right in and start canceling things on the basis of your word." She raised her chin, just as he'd known she would, and he felt that same spooky tinge of déjà vu, of destiny. He shook his head, hard.

"It may be my word, but it's also the truth," he said, gazing deep into her beautiful brown eyes. He steeled himself against the baffling waves of recognition and affection that swept over him, forging ahead, speaking sharply in an effort to convince himself more than her. "I'm sorry, Saskia, but I have to tell you that my family will never accept the idea of every poltergeist-hunting wacko on the eastern seaboard marching through our parlor. There may still be valuable items in this house." He didn't mention his precious bronzes, but he was thinking about them. "The idea of a houseful of tourists tripping over our property—not to mention *paying* to desecrate our family name—"

"Look," she said abruptly, "you might as well stop the tirade, because nothing is going to be decided tonight."

"So what are you suggesting?"

"I'm willing to put you up for the night, so that we can discuss this more calmly in the morning."

"The perfect suggestion." It was what he was getting to himself; he just hadn't had the chance yet.

But now that the offer was on the table, he felt a curious sense of foreboding. Why? "You aren't planning any tricks overnight, are you?"

"What kind of tricks did you have in mind?" she asked, clearly surprised.

He honestly didn't have any idea. He'd just been struck with the notion—out of the blue—that sleeping over at Wynnwood was a risky proposition for him. But where had that idea come from? He certainly wasn't afraid of ghosts. What could he possibly have to fear, even if he was stuck in this creepy mansion with a couple of crazy old ladies while Mother Nature was on the rampage just beyond the doors?

As he asked himself that question, thunder and lightning crashed outside, and the lamp on the mantel flickered wildly, as if it were trying to send him some kind of signal.

"I-I'd better get some candles," Saskia said uneasily. "I'm not sure about this storm."

But as she turned to go, he lay a restraining hand on her arm. He was too mesmerized by everything else that had already happened to be surprised by the strong, tangible arc of electricity that leapt between them.

Saskia glanced down at his hand where it rested against her warm, soft skin. Her eyes were round with astonishment.

"Have we...? she began.

"What?"

"Do I know...?" But she broke off, shook her head, and moved away from him in a rush. "No, of course I don't."

Stubbornly refusing to look at him, she rounded up her aunts and steered them over to the door. "Come on, darlings. Time for bed. Way past time."

"But, Saskia—" they protested.

"No buts. Come on—let's go. And you stay here," she tossed back at him over her shoulder. "I'm going up with them, but then I'll be back to discuss where we're going to put you for the night."

And then she departed, leaving him alone in the parlor with the steady drone of Madame Renata's snoring. He ran a hasty hand through his hair, trying to wake up, trying to shake some sense into himself, trying to knock himself out of this bizarre world of impulse and intuition, where memories of Saskia danced just out of his reach, where he suffered from a mysterious fear of gloomy old houses.

He was never, ever given to flights of fancy. So why had he started now?

Chapter Three

Saskia was about to have a heart attack. She needed an aspirin. She needed to lie down.

She gazed down at her arm, which was still tingling where he'd touched her. Bizarre. She honestly couldn't imagine why she was so easily rattled, so easily stirred, by the man. It was almost as if he *were* a ghost, given her reaction to him, chock-full of trembling hands and weak knees.

At this point, a part of her would've preferred he were from the spirit world. At least a ghost wouldn't have the power to throw her out on her fanny, dashing all her dreams of financial independence.

"Financial independence," she moaned, deathly afraid it was all going to go up in smoke, just because Connor Wynn and his hoity-toity relatives had decided to take an unreasonable dislike to poltergeists.

Could any of this be true? Could she possibly have sunk every dime she owned and a few she didn't into a house to which she had no claim?

She definitely needed that aspirin. She also needed to get that strange, devastating, haunting man out of here before he drove her out of her mind.

"I want him out of my house," she muttered.

Except it might not be her house.

"Darlings, you have to tell me," she said as she herded her aunts upstairs and toward to the north end of the hall. "Do you remember seeing any kind of deed or papers about Wynnwood? When you were notified about Poppy's... passing, did anyone say anything about the house and how it fit into the estate?"

"Petey Woodlawn, that nice lawyer boy, handled it all for us. Didn't he, Primrose?"

"Oh, yes, indeed. Besides, Saskia, if there were any complications, you'd have been the one to deal with them, not us," Primrose said with a sniff.

That was true enough. She supposed it was her own fault for not checking into things more carefully, but good grief! Poppy had lived in the house since 1955. Who knew there was any reason to suppose it wasn't hers?

When Aunt Poppy died and the aunts came down to arrange the funeral, it seemed the most natural thing in the world to move into Poppy's empty house. After all, Poppy's will had quite clearly left everything she owned to be divided equally between her two surviving sisters. They'd all assumed that included the house, and no one had told them any differently. Until now.

Banquo flashed in front of her, skittering on the slippery hardwood floor of the upstairs hallway. He was a very black cat, and he had just crisscrossed her path three or four times. Extremely bad luck.

But how could her luck get any worse? What was worse than meeting up with the likes of arrogant, overwhelming Connor Wynn in the dead of night, and suddenly being engulfed with feelings she had no idea how to handle?

What was worse than losing her house?

She had invested everything she owned into making something of Wynnwood. And that investment was emotional as well as financial.

Although they didn't want to admit it, the aunts were getting on in years. Never exactly paragons of responsibility or hard work, Petunia and Primrose had gotten more and more careless over the past year or so, until Saskia had become increasingly worried about their ability to run their store. And once the decision was made to give up the shop, the aunts could hardly live in the tiny apartment above it.

At the time, Wynnwood had seemed to be the only solution. It still did.

In front of Saskia, Primrose scooped up the black cat and sailed into her bedroom. Petunia was right behind her, leaving Saskia alone to ponder the gravity of their situation.

Given his reaction to an innocent bit of ghost-hunting, she could just see Connor Wynn's face when he found out that the women living in the high-and-mighty Wynn family home had spent their lives running a witches' boutique. At Something Wicked, the shelves were lined with titles such as *Pagan Rituals for Fun and Profit* and *Hexes for Every Occasion*.

She smiled grimly. Connor was going to pitch a fit.

Saskia's aunts were not exactly witches, although it wasn't for lack of trying. As long as she'd known them, they'd been practicing spells and incantations and mixing up ghastly potions and brews. No matter how miserably they flopped as sorcerers, they still had fun trying.

They'd almost burned down their store several times, so it was really a godsend to get the house on Jekyll Island, where they had more room to spread out and less chance of catastrophe. Or at least Saskia had hoped there was less chance of a catastrophe. The aunts were pretty good at finding trouble wherever they went.

So when the time came, when Poppy died and the house was theirs for the taking, Saskia had given up her job as a sometimes waitress/sometimes chef at a small caterer's, and moved all three of them into Wynnwood. Running the place as a bed-and-breakfast, Saskia had envisioned utilizing her own modest cooking talents as well as being able to keep a closer eye on the accident-prone Truelove sisters. Besides, she'd figured Petunia and Primrose would fit right in, adding color and authenticity to her haunted-house theme.

But right now, all of her plans were hanging by a thread. If Connor Wynn was telling the truth, and she had a very bad feeling he was, catastrophe was looming large for all of the Trueloves.

And catastrophe didn't begin to describe the rest of this mystifying situation—where a very normal young man walked into her house, and suddenly Saskia was reeling from sensory overload of a very odd variety. She had never had these peculiar feelings before, as if she and Connor were very well acquainted, and it had somehow slipped her mind. Until now.

"Saskia, dear, are you not feeling well?" Primrose asked kindly, peeking back out into the hall. "You're looking a bit pale."

"I imagine it's all the excitement," her sister noted. "One doesn't meet a full-blown manifestation from the spirit world every night, after all. Isn't it marvelous? Our very first séance, and such a rousing success."

"You know very well, both of you," Saskia snapped, "that Mr. Wynn is no manifestation." The ferocity of her response surprised all three of them, since she wasn't usually given to angry outbursts, especially when her aunts were in earshot. But she couldn't seem to stop herself. "He's a real person! A very ordinary real person," she insisted. "Nothing unusual at all!"

"I think he's the ghost of the Commodore," Primrose said stubbornly. She closed her door sharply without giving Saskia a chance to disagree one last time.

"Whatever he is, he's hardly ordinary. He's very handsome, isn't he?" Petunia asked, her dark eyes twinkling. "You know," she cooed, "Wynns and Trueloves match up very nicely. Just think of Poppy and Bunky."

Saskia still steamed, but she refrained from mentioning that Poppy and Bunky's union had not turned out all that well, given Bunky's unfortunate run-in with the birdbath.

Instead, she gave Aunt Petunia a quick good-night kiss and ushered her into her room. Feeling satisfied that her aunts were properly settled in, Saskia made her way back down the west hallway to the main stairs. She wished just once her aunts would straighten up and behave themselves like adults, like other people's rational, sane relatives. But she knew in her heart that was a pipe dream.

As she descended ever closer to the parlor, the thunder outside began to rumble ominously, getting on her nerves all over again. She really was on edge tonight, all out of proportion to the storm.

But ever since Connor had arrived, she'd had this dreadful feeling that something very important and very scary was just about to happen. It was as if Fate were jumping up and biting her on the nose.

Whatever was going to happen next, she knew in her heart she had no choice but to confront it. And so she pushed open the parlor door, ready to match wits with Connor Wynn.

Come into my parlor, said the spider to the fly...

Connor stood in front of the fireplace, intent on nudging the frame a quarter of an inch this way or that, so that the portrait of his great-grandfather would hang perfectly square above the mantel. Looking him up and down, Saskia shivered, and it was not from the cold. It was anything but chilly in this humid, rain-soaked air.

She fanned her face, wishing the storm clouds would blow away, that the heat, the humidity and all this violent electricity would vanish into the night.

But it wasn't going anywhere. Not while Connor was still around, still letting off enough raw current to light up the entire island.

Like his great-grandfather, Connor had thick chestnut-colored hair, cut short and pushed away from his face, and intense, crystal blue eyes. Even in the painting, those eyes looked right through you.

They had the same fierce, lowered brows, the same firmly clenched jaw, the same elegant, chiseled features. No doubt about it, the Commodore and his great-grandson were both absolutely gorgeous.

She tried to convince herself that this resounding echo of recognition came from having stared too many times at the portrait, but she knew it was a lie. The man who struck all the right chords was the living, breathing version.

Splotches of water had drenched through his button-down shirt and his dark trousers, plastering the fabric to his body here and there. His hair was slick with moisture, and small droplets clung to his brow. In this heat, it was almost as if steam were rising from him.

A small leather bag lay at his feet. Apparently, he'd gotten wet braving the elements to bring in his toothbrush and his pajamas.

Moving in already... It was not a comforting thought.

She wondered if she'd feel less anxious around him if he weren't quite so handsome. She doubted it. Even without the good looks, there was something about him, something that jangled her nerves and sent her pulse pounding.

The temperature in the stuffy room rose even higher, as Saskia tried hard to keep herself from swooning right there.

Nonsense, she told herself. It was just the excitement of the evening, just surprise and shock at the way he'd blown in through the french doors on the wings of the tempest.

Of course she was frazzled. Who wouldn't be under these circumstances?

Angrily, she wiped the back of her hand across her moist forehead. "Mr. Wynn," she began, and when he turned to meet her, she jumped back. She couldn't help it. She had forgotten that he was even more devastating when those blue eyes were looking right at her.

He lifted a bronze eyebrow. "Yes?"

"I, uh . . ." She had completely forgotten what she planned to say. "I've decided it's definitely better to discuss this all tomorrow."

"Didn't we already decide that?"

"Well, yes, but I'm just reiterating it."

She cut a wide berth around him on her way to the french doors, where she double-checked the latches. They seemed secure enough. So how had he gotten in?

Maybe he wafted right through the wall.

"Besides," she went on, jiggling the handle back and forth, "I don't have any of the right paperwork, or any way to get it tonight. So I can't refute anything you say until I can talk to my aunts' lawyer and get a look at all the papers."

"You won't be able to refute anything anyway." He sneaked up behind her, much too close for comfort, and then reached all the way around her. "If you're trying to lock it, you have to turn the dead bolt the other way."

She snatched her hand away as he dealt with the lock, neatly flipping it into place, but she could still feel the energy and the steam emanating from his big, hard, wet body. She was so keyed up, so easily provoked. And yet she had this outrageous need to close her eyes and give in, to curl up in his lap and start purring. Yet his lap was the last thing she ought to be thinking about. Damn the man.

Trapped between him and the cool glass, Saskia tried to maintain her dignity. "Are you always this handy, or is it just with french doors?"

Berating him about his prowess with doors—good grief, she sounded like an idiot.

At her back, she could feel the pane rattling as the rain beat against it from outside. Thunder and lightning, crashing waves, high winds and pouring rain—all the bad omens that had accompanied Connor's dramatic entrance were back out in full force.

He smiled, but he didn't move. His eyes were very blue as he stared down at her. "At least you're admitting this *is* a Wynn family home."

"All I'm admitting is what it used to be." Saskia ducked under his arm and escaped to the other side of the parlor, with a table and four chairs in between them, where she could breathe more freely.

He let her go, but his gaze followed her closely, and she felt almost as uneasy as she had right in his clutches. "What a mess," she said heartily, and she made a swipe at collecting the various candles and cleaning up the cake plate. She wondered vaguely where Madame Renata had gotten to, although she supposed it really didn't matter, as long as the psychic hadn't collapsed under the table or something.

As if reading her mind, Connor chose that moment to announce, "If you're looking for Madame Renata, she's on the sofa in the other parlor. She passed out on the chair in here, so I carried her in there."

Saskia's eyes widened. "You carried her?"

She hadn't expected him to start toting her guests around. Her mind flashed to an image of Madame Renata, limp and dazed, securely bundled in Connor's strong embrace.

Some people have all the luck, don't they? her traitorous brain asked her. *And wouldn't those be wonderful arms to get caught up in?*

"No, they wouldn't," she said under her breath.

"Wouldn't what?" When she offered no response, he shrugged. "It seemed as good an idea as any. I think she's probably out for the night."

"Thank you. That was very kind of you."

Connor smiled. "Well, I didn't know what else to do with her."

His eyes held her, and she felt warm and flushed all of a sudden, as if he had read her mind—again—and knew that she was fantasizing about being swept down the halls of Wynnwood in his powerful embrace, as if that very thing had happened before.

But of course it had never happened before!

What was wrong with her? Moreover, what was wrong with him? "It's getting late," she said quickly. "I guess I should put you to bed."

"Excuse me?"

Hot color suffused her cheeks. Had she really said that? "I mean, I can show you to your room. Luckily, several are already in good shape, ready for when we open as a bed-and-breakfast, I mean." Wheeling, she got out of there before she made a more serious verbal blunder.

I should put you to bed... Oh, Lord. The mental images *that* created were not to be believed. Her body, his body, soft covers, cool linens, flickering candles... The pictures in her mind were so clear and so intoxicating, it was impossible to say that they were fantasy, not memory.

Outrageous.

She steeled herself to be strong, no matter how late the hour, no matter how strange and provocative the atmosphere. "This way, Mr. Wynn."

He trailed along behind her. "Please, call me Connor."

"Actually," she announced, stopping with her hand on the big newel post at the bottom of the stairs, "I'd just as soon not make friends with you while you're dead set on taking away my aunts' house."

It had nothing to do with the house, really, but she had this overwhelming need to put him in his place. Maybe it wasn't his fault that she was all wrought up and imagining things about his arms and his bed. But she needed to do something before she lost her mind, and building a wall between them seemed like the best idea at the moment. She went with the impulse.

"So I'd just as soon keep things at the Mr. Wynn stage, if that's all right with you."

He paused, meeting her gaze. Finally, he said coolly, "Fair enough."

Saskia felt she had made her point, but it didn't make the long trip up the stairs and along the second-floor hallway any easier. She could feel his rapt gaze, burning a hole in her back the entire way.

"Here," she said with relief, ushering him into a large bedroom at the end of the west hall. "The Poppy Suite."

This had been the first part of the house refurbished, and in honor of Aunt Poppy, it was dark and dramatic. Formerly the master bedroom, it had a big bed, an attached sitting room, and its own bath. Saskia expected it to be her most expensive accommodation.

Because it was so large, it was rather sparsely furnished, but it was done up very comfortably and elegantly, nonetheless. It featured Poppy's signature flower everywhere—blooming across the wallpaper, lacquered onto the drawers of the highboy, needle-pointed on the bench at the foot of the bed, even worked into the heavy curtains around the four-poster.

"Not very restful, is it?" he asked, gazing around at the blaze of red and black. There was an edge to his voice when he asked, "Are you trying to give me nightmares about dear, departed Aunt Poppy?"

"Of course not." But now that she thought about it, it wasn't such a bad idea. Maybe he could dredge up a little guilt over the idea of displacing Poppy's relatives while he was here. "You should find everything you need," she said sweetly. "I'll see you in the morning."

"Don't you think it's awfully hot in here?" he asked, already unbuttoning his cuffs, opening his collar, flapping the front of his shirt back and forth.

She bit her lip, hard. Connor Wynn starting to undress in front of her was more ammunition than she needed for some disturbing dreams of her own.

She backed toward the door, mumbling, "I'm sorry about the heat. I'm afraid the air-conditioning doesn't seem to do too well in the west wing." She hastened to add, "But we can open the window if you want to, although I don't think the air from outside is all that cool, either."

He pushed open the window, just far enough to see that it was still raining heavily. "Wouldn't want to ruin my woodwork," he said sardonically, shoving it back shut. "Do you think you could find me a fan?"

"I can try."

He ran a hand through his hair. "Good. Just leave it outside the door, all right?"

He sounded positively testy. So he didn't want her making extra trips into his bedroom. Well, that was fine with her.

"Good night, Mr. Wynn." She slid out the door, but turned back far enough to offer, "I'm sure we'll work everything out to our mutual satisfaction in the morning."

His lips settled into a hard line. "I'm sure we will."

Saskia knew when it was wise to retreat. As she made tracks down the hall, on the way to dig up a fan, she promised herself that she would be able to control herself—and him—much better by morning.

She had almost reached the main staircase, musing on where in the house an extra fan might be hiding, when she began to smell a very suspicious odor.

It smelled vaguely like vegetable soup. Or maybe some strange variety of tea. A splash of tarragon, a promise of oregano...all overlaid with cinnamon and roses. This tantalizing, overwhelming aroma wafted into her nostrils, beckoning her upstairs. To the attic.

"Oh, no," she whispered. She knew that smell, that mixture of herbs and spices and exotic perfumes....

Her aunts couldn't have picked a worse time to start brewing up witchcraft again.

Chapter Four

As quietly as she could manage, Saskia crept up the spindly stairs to the attic.

If they knew she was coming, there was a good chance they'd knock their pots over and set the whole place on fire, in their haste to cover up the evidence of their witches' brew. That's what had almost happened the last time, and she didn't want to risk it again.

When she got to the place on the stairs where the attic floor was at eye level, she stopped, peering into the dim space. Her gaze ran smack-dab into a pair of spooky, slanted yellow eyes.

She jumped back, her heart pounding, until she realized what she'd seen. "Banquo," she whispered. "You almost gave me a heart attack."

The cat slithered away, over by an incense burner sitting on the floor a foot or so from the steps. It reeked of attar of roses.

Roses... Weren't they supposed to accompany love potions and charms? But surely Primrose and Petunia weren't looking for lovers at this late date? The two of them were decidedly past their prime. Besides, they knew as well as anyone that the Truelove women were cursed in matters of the heart. Her aunts were more superstitious than most, and they took the Truelove curse very seriously.

The smell of the incense mingled with a different odor, coming from what looked like a fondue pot, plugged into an extension cord on the floor nearby. Whatever was in there was boiling away, and it smelled like tomato soup.

Saskia frowned. They were using an electric fondue pot, when they knew they weren't supposed to have things plugged in up here. She supposed this meant she was going to have to do the fire-safety lecture again, and she hated that kind of thing. It just wasn't in her to be stern and disapproving, although heaven knew she tried.

From her vantage point, she couldn't see either of her aunts, but she could hear them rustling around. Quietly, she eased farther up into the attic, careful to stay in the shadows as she blew out the incense and unplugged the fondue pot, eliminating two hazards with one fell swoop.

Now she could see Petunia and Primrose straight ahead. Both were wearing long white nightgowns as they rustled around a small, square table covered with a lacy cloth. The floor around them was littered with stacks of books—short, fat ones, oversize thin ones, plain ones, fancy ones—all kinds of dusty, musty tomes. It looked as if they'd been leafing through every book they owned, searching for just the right spell.

Petunia stood at the table, carefully laying out a variety of candles and other strange things that looked like small tree branches and colored stones. Behind her, with her hair unbound nearly to her waist, Primrose was singing softly to herself and keeping time with a tambourine.

Saskia sighed. Just yesterday they'd promised they weren't going to try to cast any more spells. The promise hadn't even lasted twenty-four hours. They were incorrigible.

As Saskia watched, not sure whether to interfere or just observe, Petunia asked, "Are you ready, Primmy?"

"Here I go." Taking a deep breath, Primrose began to chant on a vague sort of "lalala" theme, smacking her tambourine around at random.

Petunia took that as her cue, lighting two fat white candles as she intoned, "Candles burn with fire bright. Goddess lead us with your light."

Primrose started leaping around more vigorously, picking up the volume of her "lala" chant, and almost stepping on Banquo in the process. The big black cat squealed and ran for cover under the tablecloth.

Petunia's sleeve dangled perilously close to a candle flame, and Saskia braced herself for a rescue effort, but her aunt snatched it out of the way at the last minute as she merrily lit another one, a thin pink taper this time. Petunia waited until it was blazing brightly, and then she picked up a branch of pussy willow, setting the branch in a silver dish in the center of the table and setting that on fire, too.

Finally, the old lady cried, "Wax will melt and willow weep. Love for Saskia we must reap."

Saskia's eyes shot open wider. A love spell for *her?* She should've known.

Hadn't Petunia been spouting nonsense about Connor being handsome, and Wynns and Trueloves matching up well? It all presaged something exactly like this. When her aunts got ideas in their heads, no matter how silly, there was no deterring them.

Of course, it didn't matter. Saskia knew very well that her aunts together wielded about as much magical power as a burned-out light bulb.

But still... This sort of thing made her nervous. Especially if any one of those candles happened to fall over onto a stack of old books, and started a conflagration of Biblical proportions.

For the first time, she noticed Banquo, poking his head out from under the table and sinking his claws into the fringe on the tablecloth. The cat was yanking down on the cloth, which was going to come crashing down any minute, bringing all those candles with it.

Saskia gulped, grabbing the fondue pot, ready to spring into action and douse the fire with the liquid potion, but Primrose chose that moment to cha-cha over and swat the cat away, all the while keeping time with her tambourine. One disaster averted, and Saskia sighed with relief.

Petunia paid no attention to any of it. Waving her hands above the flames, she yelled, "Candle rose before candle red—burn visions of true love in Connor's head."

She'd been expecting it, but it was still entirely too eerie to hear out loud, especially in Petunia's bright, cheerful voice. Her aunt said it again, louder, and Saskia's nerve endings jangled like an untuned piano.

He was the last man on earth she wanted to get stuck with. And he was the last man on earth who needed extra spells to stoke her fire.

But Primrose continued to chant and spin around as Petunia called, "Knotted together these two must be." She tied a dusty rose ribbon into a bow around the two fat white candles. "Passion bind them through eternity."

Saskia's head began to spin. *Knotted together these two must be; passion bind them through eternity....* The words whirled in her brain with dizzying speed.

Primrose's dancing and tambourine suddenly gained new energy, and her sister threw caution to the winds, lighting a whole circle of deep red candles, tossing handfuls of sparkly powders into the silver dish.

Petunia hollered, "Himminy pimminy walaboo weesh—a storm of passion we unleash! Hobbledy gobbledy malakah maim—desire will dazzle the two we name!"

Primrose joined in. "Saskia Truelove and Connor Wynn! In their hearts, let love begin!"

The things in the dish were casting sparks, the candles were flaming higher and higher, and Saskia felt faint. When had it gotten so hot in the attic?

Her aunts kept chanting on about storms of passion and dazzling desire, until she couldn't stand it anymore. With her hands over her ears, she shouted, "Stop this right now!"

"Oh, hello, dear," Petunia offered brightly. "Don't knock anything over, will you? We're in the middle of something."

"I know." Slowly the light and the heat seemed to recede, and Saskia felt her reason return.

"Did you see the whole thing?" Petunia inquired. "It was all quite exciting."

"My dance went very well, I thought. Very well," Primrose added.

Weakly, Saskia held up the fondue pot by the handle. "I unplugged your potion." She peered down into the pot. "Was it for me?"

Petunia blinked. "No, dear, it's vegetable soup. Casting spells always makes us hungry."

"Well, that's a relief."

"Did you douse the incense, too?" Primrose asked fretfully. "I do hope that doesn't interfere with the potency of the spell."

"I wouldn't worry about it if I were you," Saskia said darkly. She marched over and blew out all the candles on the table, pinching the wicks to make sure they were out for good.

"You know, Primrose, Saskia is right. I'm sure it was plenty potent," Petunia remarked in a jolly little voice. "It felt so very strong and lusty when I was casting it."

Lusty? That didn't sound like anything that ought to be coming from Petunia.

"Did you like the incantation?" Petunia asked eagerly.

"It was quite impressive," Saskia managed. "Although you really—"

But Petunia had already turned away to talk to her co-conspirator, ignoring Saskia completely. "She's taking it very well, isn't she, sister? I told you not to fuss. All she needed was a push."

"I was quite anxious, you see," Primrose confided, "about the Truelove curse and all, that we shouldn't try to snare you someone, if he'll just die as soon as you've got him. That hardly seems fair."

Saskia was having a hard time following this. "Because of Bunky and the birdbath, you mean?"

"Well, that and your own father," Petunia put in. "Although we didn't really like Maurice, he *was* your father, and we would never have wished him ill."

"But he didn't die. He just divorced my mother and ran off with the model who'd posed for those horrid nude paintings he was so fond of."

"Artists," Primrose grumbled. "Simply can't be trusted. Nevertheless, we're all well aware there is a curse on Truelove women. We are not fated to succeed with affairs of the heart."

Petunia added, "And we also weren't certain that you would care for being matched up with Mr. Wynn. He isn't really your sort of boy, Saskia, dear. On the surface, of course. But we feel quite certain that underneath all that stuffy, repressive bluster, he's exactly the right one. Quite certain. Isn't that right, Primmy?"

"Oh, yes, certainly. Although he is rather gloomy, isn't he?"

"But you know, Primmy, frivolity by itself is no guarantee that a young man will be suitable. Why, think of Maurice. He was as bohemian as they come, and yet he was quite the wrong man for Pansy."

"Quite," Petunia agreed.

"It all depends on the cosmic forces at work, and those are very tricky to predict. Don't fret, though, because there's plenty of sexual energy here. We sense that." Petunia chewed her fingernail daintily, as Saskia felt her own cheeks flame with embarrassment. "What we're not quite so sure of is his spiritual capacity. But we think that can be developed. In time."

What with all this talk of sexual energy, Saskia wondered suddenly if her aunts had picked up on the murky chemistry swimming in the air between her and Connor. Normally she would've sworn they were too preoccupied with their own fantasy world to notice anything she did, but maybe it was *so* obvious this time that even the space-cadet Truelove sisters had seen it.

Was her libido that obvious? What a frightening notion.

"And why exactly did you decided to cast this spell?" she asked quickly.

"Well, we thought we could block the curse," Petunia offered. "A preemptive strike, so to speak."

"And then there's the house," her sister added. "If it really is his, he might make us leave. And we really do like it here so very much. You see that, don't you, dear? Being close to Poppy and everything, we would simply hate to leave Wynnwood."

At her elbow, Petunia nodded and smiled sweetly. "But if you're married to Mr. Wynn, then we can stay. It all makes perfect sense, and it solves our problems very neatly."

Saskia was speechless. She had worried that they were too fragile to absorb the bad news about Wynnwood, but somewhere along the line they'd absorbed it in a heartbeat. And then they'd immediately gotten down to brass tacks, making plans—that made sense to them, if no one else—on how to foil Connor and secure their position.

All before Saskia had even had time to catch her breath.

"And besides," Petunia went on, "he's a very nice-looking young man, and you *are* getting a bit long in the tooth, dear. We thought he would make an excellent match for you, in a stodgy sort of way."

Aside from the fact that she had been apprehensive about their reactions, and frightened of her own reaction to Connor, there was something irritating about all this. Her *own* aunts felt the need to burn candles and chant crazy rhymes to get her a man. It was humiliating.

Was she so hideous, so hopeless, that she couldn't attract Connor—or any other man—the regular way?

Not that she wanted to. Not even a little. But still...

If she *had* wanted to, she would've preferred to depend on her own personal charms, rather than candles and chants and intervention from goddesses. This way was for social rejects, for nutty people who felt they had no hope of getting along in the world without the aid of the supernatural. Saskia had never thought of herself that way.

She was starting to become rather miffed with her aunts, but one look at their sweet faces deflated her anger. Saskia could never really be all that mad at them.

They might be irresponsible and odd, but they meant well. Besides, they had taken her in when her mother died, when there was no one else, and she could never repay that debt.

"I really don't think trying to match me up with Connor is going to solve anything," she said finally. That much at least was true. Especially since she had the distinct feeling that getting anywhere near Connor was a disastrous idea for her own well-being. "But thank you for your concern."

"Of course, dear," Petunia told her.

Carelessly knocking books every which way, Primrose started packing away all the stones and powders laid out on the table, but she looked up with a troubled expression when she heard Saskia's words. "Does that mean we shouldn't go forward with our plans for Mr. Wynn?"

"What plans?" Saskia asked with a certain sense of foreboding.

"Oh, nothing," Petunia said blandly, waving signals at her sister to be quiet.

Saskia had experienced enough of their dreadful potions and charms to be very wary of inflicting anything on anyone else. "You have to promise me you won't do anything to Connor."

She could just imagine his reaction if he caught Primrose snipping locks of his hair to make into a voodoo doll, or sneaking eye of newt or leg of lizard into his breakfast cereal.

"Please, promise me you'll leave him alone," she tried again. It was all silliness, of course—her aunts had never come close to succeeding with any of their abracadabra nonsense in the past, even by accident—but she really didn't want to risk poisoning Connor.

"Of course." But Petunia's gaze was wandering all around the rafters. "If that's what you want, dear."

Petunia was vague enough to really worry Saskia. Who knew what they had up their sorcerers' sleeves?

"Listen to me, you two," she said sternly. "No tricks, no potions, no spells—nothing to do with Connor. And tomorrow we need to have a serious talk about using electrical appliances in the attic. It's very dangerous."

Petunia smiled sweetly as Primrose scraped wax off the tablecloth. Neither one of them was paying the slightest attention. What was she going to do with them?

She finally gave up and left them eating their soup off the white tablecloth, swearing they would go right to bed as soon as they were done. Surely they couldn't get into any more trouble in one evening?

With Banquo dogging her steps, Saskia slipped back down the attic steps and into the second floor hall. Everything seemed quiet enough.

It was also very hot, which reminded her of what she was doing when she'd been interrupted by all the hocus-pocus upstairs. Connor was melting and cranky and needed a fan.

And so she went back to her fan-hunting expedition, locating one eventually in the closet of the Daffodil bedroom in the north wing.

Toting the fan, feeling tired enough to keel over, she retraced her steps to Connor's room one more time. She had every intention of dropping the fan outside his door and maybe quietly knocking once or twice, just to let him know it was there if he needed it.

But as she stooped to leave the fan, she heard the most amazing noises coming from inside.

She knelt, pressing her eye to the keyhole, as Banquo nestled at her feet, meowing plaintively. "Sssh," she told him. But all she could see through the keyhole was deep, inky darkness. Switching her ear to the hole, she had better luck. She could hear moaning and groaning, tossing and turning, as if there were a whole shipload full of seasick people in there.

Was that the floor, or the bed creaking like that? And what was making that terrible bumping and thumping noise?

What was going on in there?

She was suddenly gripped with the horrifying notion that Connor knew her aunts had tried to tie him up in a big, nasty spell, and he was in there right now trying to physically fight off the spell, like wrestling a lion.

"Oh, come on, there's no way he could know about the spell unless he went up to the attic, too," she muttered, but she just couldn't get the idea out of her head that there was something very wrong here, and it was somehow her fault.

Finally, after several anxious moments with her ear pressed to his door, Saskia could stand it no longer. She turned the knob.

It was unlocked.

At first, she just slid it open an inch or two. "Connor?" she called out softly, putting one foot into the darkness of his room. "Are you okay?"

She could make out his general form over there on the heavy four-poster, rolling around as if he were in the middle of a gymnastic exercise. That accounted for the moans and groans, as well as the bumps and squeaks, since he was practically lifting the bed off the floor as he thrashed back and forth.

He definitely seemed to be asleep, although how he could sleep through *this* was beyond her. She felt a little guilty, actually. She might have wished a few inconsequential guilt-inducing nightmares on him, something where Poppy raised her ghostly arms and commanded him to run away from Wynnwood and never come back. But this was ridiculous.

"Connor?" she asked again, venturing closer. "I think you're having a bad dream. Either that or you have malaria," she muttered. She seemed to remember Errol Flynn exhibiting this sort of reaction to some tropical disease on the late, late show. "Wake up, Connor," she said gently. "It's just a dream. Wake up."

But her words had no effect on him whatsoever. The nearer she got, the more of him she could see, and the clearer it became that he was definitely not awake.

It was also clear that his bedroom was a hazardous place for her to be.

Perspiration glistened against his forehead, on his shoulders, down over the muscles of his bare, smooth chest. The bedclothes were flung every which way, with only a red sheet wrapping him at the waist, dipping lower and lower as he tossed and turned.

Her mouth went dry, but she couldn't take her eyes off him. The man was gorgeous. The man was half-naked.

She swore out loud, as her blood pounded in her veins and her hands clasped and unclasped, aching to touch him. He was gorgeous and half-naked, and she wanted to run her hands over all that hot, slippery, bare skin.

Okay, so it wasn't really fair to stand there and stare at him when he was obviously suffering from a terrifying nightmare, but what could she do?

Okay, so it was really stupid to stand there and devour him with her eyes when she already knew he was dangerous and arrogant, when she already knew he exerted some powerful pull over her that she couldn't explain or resist. But at the moment it wasn't in her to walk away.

The man was gorgeous. The man was half-naked. Or maybe *all* naked under that sheet.

And her mind went wild with the possibilities.

She was no saint, after all. Trying to remember to breathe, she leaned forward very slowly, setting an unsteady hand on his hard forearm, sizzling her fingers where she touched him.

"Ohh," she moaned. He felt wonderful.

"Darling, is that you?" he asked fuzzily.

"Darling? Uh, no. No, I don't think so," she tried, but it was too late.

Connor's strong arm snaked out and reeled her in. Before she knew what hit her, Saskia was wedged underneath him, trapped by his body in that big, soft bed.

Chapter Five

It was bliss. It was torture.

Her brain was telling her to run while she still had the chance, but her body wasn't cooperating.

She did manage to gather her wits enough to try to wiggle out from under his grasp, but that only made things worse. The wrong things wiggled against the wrong things, and she knew she was in big trouble. Her temperature began to rise. Her body seemed to melt. Saskia lay very still.

Above her, Connor smiled drowsily, murmuring endearments, nuzzling her neck, angling closer and pulling her hard up against his long, strong body. He stared down into her eyes, his own gaze soft and dreamy, with a glimmer of a lazy grin curving his narrow lips.

"You are so very beautiful, my love," he whispered.

"Connor, please," she said woozily. Was she asking him to stop? Or go further? She had no idea. But when his mouth found the nape of her neck, she knew it was warm and wonderful.

Warm wasn't the word for it. The man was radiating enough heat for a five-alarm fire, singeing her where she lay. His skin felt smooth, slick and unbearably hot under her fingers. She was starting to smolder herself, just from the proximity.

What did she think she was doing?

But, my, oh, my... With his strong arms around her and his hard body pressing her down into the bed it was impossible to resist. Whatever faint tremor of recognition had teased her before had now turned into an absolute avalanche of memory and desire. The heady aroma of the love potion—a major case of déjà vu, a conflagration of candles burning out of control—her head spun with the blur of images and emotions. What was all this? It was as if she were drowning in a sea of destiny.

But there was no time to wonder.

She was partially tangled in his sheet, enfolded in his arms as he nibbled her earlobe and ran soft kisses along the line of her chin. "Oh, that feels fabulous," she mumbled. "But why... why are you doing this?"

"When a lady enters a gentleman's bedchamber at this hour of night, it is not difficult to ascertain her intentions," he said darkly, giving her a wicked smile as he tightened his embrace, lifting her slightly, wrapping her even more securely in his arms.

He was so close and so warm, and she was so vulnerable. But somewhere, in the last rational corner of her brain, she heard the words "bedchamber" and "ascertain" and she thought vaguely that he didn't sound like himself at all.

"My darling child, I knew you would come to me tonight," he whispered.

"Darling child? Tonight? But how did you know?"

"No need for your pretty little objections now, my love." He kissed her quick and hard, leaving her breathless and hungry. "Between us, there is no need for words."

"Between us?"

At the moment, there was precious little between them, except for one dangerously rumpled sheet and the soft cotton of her dress, which was hiking higher every time Connor twisted her around in the bed. His body was as hot as a pistol, blasting right through the fabric of her dress, and she was becoming more and more sure that he wasn't wearing anything at all.

Oh, God. It was too tempting for words to just knock the sheet away and feel all of him, bare and strong and perfect.

She wanted him to kiss her again, to drug her with the sweetness of his lips, but instead he pulled back, and his expression was darker, more dangerous.

"I fear I have given in too easily. You have led me a pretty dance, my love," he said roughly. "I have waited a long time for you to come to your senses. Perhaps I ought to make you wait as I have."

"A-a long time?"

"All these weeks," he whispered, "as I've waited for you to come to me, I've seen the promise in your mysterious smile and the light in your enchanting eyes. I knew what you felt in your heart, even if you refused to give in, my intoxicating little minx."

"What promise? What light?" His words were so strangely phrased—and he was talking as if they'd met weeks ago, instead of just a few hours before. It was hard to think at all, with the imprint of his kiss still on her lips and the feel of his arms so hard around her, but she knew this wasn't right. "What light is in my eyes?" she asked warily.

He smiled again, arrogant and sure of himself. "The light of desire. Your whole body sings with it." He drew a slow finger down her cheek, tracing the outline of her lower lip, rubbing it very gently. "Your body throbs. It quivers. For me."

Any retort she might've planned died in her throat. Saskia knew with dreadful certainty that she was blushing from the inside out, bathing herself in hot, rosy color.

Where did he get words like that, words that made her want to moan and whimper? Words that made her throb and quiver, even if she hadn't even considered throbbing or quivering before?

"My darling," he whispered. "I have been waiting so long for you, from the first moment we met. I saw you across that ballroom, sipping your punch like an angel, and I knew someday you would be mine."

This was getting weirder and weirder all the time. Too odd to ignore, no matter how strongly she was tempted.

Saskia tried to collect her fevered, frantic thoughts, to pretend that she was all alone in her own cool bed, where she could think, where her skin wasn't slick with his sweat, where his hot masculine scent didn't fill her nostrils every time she breathed.

Think, she commanded herself. But no matter how hard she concentrated, none of his words made sense.

What had happened since she'd met Connor earlier that evening? He'd seemed familiar then—how she imagined it would feel to meet a long-lost lover again after years apart—but nothing like *this,* nothing like this flowery, ardent lover with his profusion of "enchanting eyes" and "mysterious smiles."

And what was that about sipping punch in a ballroom? Saskia couldn't recall ever having set foot in a ballroom, let alone one with punch.

Before, when they'd met in the parlor, he'd sounded like any normal uptight East Coast businessman of the nineties. Okay, so he was an unusually good-looking uptight businessman, and when he touched her he gave off electric shocks. But this was way beyond that. This was bizarre.

I've been waiting so long, he'd said, yet they'd only met tonight. So what in the world was he talking about?

It was as if he were suddenly a different person.

She reached up swiftly, laying her hand on his forehead. Hot as blazes. But she already knew that. Was he feverish? Hallucinating? Making love in his sleep?

"He's not asleep," she mumbled under her breath. "You have to be awake to behave like this."

"No more of your incessant chatter, my love. I know you pride yourself on your rather scarlet reputation," he said, but his smile was indulgent as his finger once again sketched a path over her cheek and her lips. "But my darling child, we both know you are a complete innocent when it comes to lovemaking, no matter how diligently you work to make the world think otherwise. But it is of no consequence." His smile took on a more provocative edge. "I am experienced enough to teach you properly."

"Teach me?" she choked. "Teach me lovemaking?"

Was this some kind of game? She caught at his hands as they started to venture a bit more boldly under the sheets. One clasped her hip, urging her closer, as the other snaked under the hem of her skirt.

"Oh, my..."

If only it didn't feel so good when he stroked her like that. He was showing off the expertise he'd been bragging about, that was for sure.

"I'm not that innocent," she tried, attempting to edge out from under him, but succeeding only in plastering herself against his chest. She could hardly breathe. "Connor, please—I just don't think you're yourself right now."

But he paid no attention, just kept nuzzling her neck and sliding his hands places they shouldn't be. "Darling," he said, in a low, intent tone that sent shivers down her spine, "I know you're apprehensive. I know you have rejected my marriage proposals time and time again. But it will be wonderful and magical between us—you'll see that. We want each other desperately. We can deny it no longer."

She tried to take in some air, to get some oxygen to her brain, but her toes were curling and her body was tingling like a house afire. Okay, so she couldn't deny she wanted him. But she could deny she wanted him *now,* this way, when he was raging about nonexistent marriage proposals.

"I think you might be sick," she said in an unsteady voice. "You're acting so strangely."

"Ah, yes, my darling, I am sick. Lovesick."

He wasn't taking no for an answer. In fact, he wasn't taking anything for an answer, and she didn't know what to do. There was a certain appeal to just giving in and letting him kiss her and caress her—oh, was that appealing—but Saskia tried to resist.

You are not this sort of person, she told herself firmly. *You can't do this with someone who doesn't seem to have the tightest grip on reality at the moment.*

But her body and her senses didn't care what objections she raised; they were enjoying themselves too much.

Reeling, she lay back and gave in to the delicious, maddening pressure of his hands. "What's happened to you, Connor?" she asked breathlessly. "What happened in the last few hours to turn you into this raging...ohh...love machine?"

And then it hit her. What had happened? How about her aunts up in the attic, churning out love potions?

"Oh, my God!"

Saskia sat up abruptly, surprising Connor enough that he sort of pitched over to one side, with a muttered "oof" noise. But she had no time for that now. Her mind was racing.

Was it possible her aunts had really done it this time? She suddenly had the terrible feeling that maybe

Petunia and Primrose knew their eye of newt from their lizard's leg after all.

Aunt Petunia's incantation spun dizzily in the air around Saskia, as clearly as if she were hearing it for the first time.

Tied together these two must be. Passion bind them through eternity....

...A storm of passion we unleash....

...Desire will dazzle the two we name....

Passion, desire... Connor was positively seething with it.

None of this explained why he was suddenly talking as if he were caught in a time warp, or why he thought she was a virgin with a bad reputation—if that was indeed what he thought, because she still wasn't sure she had his delusions straight—but maybe it was all part of the spell.

"Oh, my God," she said again.

"Darling," he mumbled, groping around in the bed for her.

"Oh, no, you don't. You touch me again and I'm a goner. So my only choice is not to let you get your hands on me."

Taking her chance, she jumped out over the side of the tall bed. She would've made it just fine, but her foot was still caught in those horrid red sheets. As she hit the floor with a thump, she yanked a whole raft of bedclothes—and Connor—down with her. They tumbled together on the floor in a jumble of limbs and linens.

"Your high spirits," he roared, "wear exceedingly thin."

But his voice died out very oddly at the end of the sentence. She could see him over there in the dim light, sitting upright in a pile of sheets, holding his head and shaking it.

"Connor?" she ventured. She had just decided her only alternative was to get away from him. Yet here she sat, wanting nothing more than to jump back into the bed with him and forget all about the obvious problems looming between them. Now that he wasn't acting so amorous, she was bereft, lonely, miserable. "Are you okay? Did you hit your head when you fell?"

"Hit my head?" he mumbled. "Fell?"

"You fell out of the bed. We both did. Are you all right?"

Connor bolted to his feet, grabbing the scarlet linen and wrapping himself toga style. "What do you mean, we fell out of the bed? What in hell were we doing in a bed? Together?"

Her mouth fell open. "You mean you don't remember?"

"Remember what?"

Saskia stood, too, making a show out of pulling down her dress and adjusting her sleeves. "You," she said pointedly, "moaning and groaning and having some kind of nightmare—and me, coming in to make sure you were okay."

"I do remember some kind of a dream...." He shook his head again, harder. "A weird dream, about pussy willows and bonfires, and red roses everywhere."

Saskia felt all the blood drain from her face. "P-pussy willows?" Her aunts had burned a branch of pussy willow. But how could Connor know that? And roses—the attic had reeked of attar of roses from the incense burner. Feeling worse and worse about this, she sat back down on the floor. "Their spell. It worked. How could they?"

Connor stalked over to the bedside table, switching on a lamp. "Look, I don't know what game you're playing, but I don't like it. A bad dream's a bad dream. Fine. But you happen to hear me having a nightmare, and then hop into bed with me?"

His face and his tone were hard and ugly, and Saskia did not appreciate the insinuation. "I was being nice!" she insisted. "Kind and considerate, because you were creating such a racket that I was afraid you might hurt yourself. So I walked over by the bed..." She proceeded more carefully, lying through her teeth so she didn't have to admit she'd stood there drooling over him. "I walked over by the bed to try to wake you up. But you reached out and grabbed me and hauled me in with you."

"I did *what?*" Connor's eyebrows shot up; his aristocratic face was a study in surprise and confusion. "I couldn't have. I would never—"

"Yes, you did," she told him. "I tried to get out from under you, but you were very persistent. You were giving me this line of goo, calling me darling and stuff, and telling me you'd waited long enough. It was..." she lifted her chin and looked him straight in the eye, with as much dignity as she could muster "...it was awful."

"I've never heard anything more ridiculous in my life," he shot back. "This is all some kind of trick, isn't it? Some scheme to confuse and humiliate me, to chase me away from here so you can keep the house."

"It is not! *You* kissed *me*. Not to mention pawing at me. And saying all these very weird things, about minxes and virgins."

His lips pressed together in a grim line. "To think I believed you when you promised you'd behave yourself until morning. You promised, Saskia. But I guess your promises don't amount to much, do they?"

"I didn't do anything," she swore. "If anybody's playing tricks, it's you."

"Somebody hopped into my bed." He cast a look down at his sheet, hoisting it into a more secure position. "And somebody stole my pajamas right off my body."

"Are you accusing me of . . . ?"

But she stopped in midquestion. Furious, Saskia marched for the door. She'd had quite enough of Connor Wynn and both of his infuriating personalities.

"I didn't steal your lousy pajamas, you moron. You weren't wearing any when I got here." She felt her cheeks grow warmer. "Or at least I don't think you were. It's not like I made sure or anything."

"Yeah, right," he grumbled.

"You are really unbelievable, you know that? As if I would be so anxious to sleep with you that I would take advantage of you while you were asleep. Why, it sounds like a Victorian novel."

"I wouldn't put it past a Truelove for five seconds."

"I really don't care what you think of the Trueloves," she returned. "I think you're a certifiable nut case, calling me an 'enchanted minx' and your 'darling child.' It's enough to make a grown woman gag."

"I called you *what?*"

"Oh, forget it. But next time you have nightmares, moan and groan at somebody else, will you?" She held her head high as she swung out the door into the hall. "Next time, I'll send Primrose or Petunia. Maybe one of them will be more interested in playing the 'little minx' part than I was."

Behind her, Connor began to cough, as if he'd swallowed the wrong way, but she was determined to leave him to his own devices. Even if it wasn't his fault. Entirely.

"I know this is a trick," he shouted after her. "I know you and your aunts are behind this. Sending me bad dreams, sending ghosts and spirits to haunt me, driving me crazy!"

Heaven help him. What if he was right?

Out in the hall, Saskia muttered a particularly colorful oath and leaned her forehead against the wall. Poor Connor was caught in the cross hairs of the first Truelove potion ever that had actually worked.

And Saskia had no idea how to get him out.

AFTER FINALLY LOCATING his pajama bottoms where they'd been tossed under the bed, Connor slipped them on in a rush, still a little wary that Saskia might come barreling back in. He couldn't quite believe she'd been here, only moments ago, wrestling on the floor with him and his bedclothes, while he wasn't wearing so much as a stitch.

It was bizarre. It was bewildering. It was downright terrifying.

He couldn't keep away the picture of Saskia sitting on the floor, with her dark curls tousled every which way, her mouth soft and kissable and her dress riding up over her thighs, revealing lots of creamy pale skin.

"Oh, Lord. I can't think about that now." Without hesitating, he wrenched open the window and stuck his head out into the downpour. As the rain spilled relentlessly over his face, he allowed himself to hope that this hard, wet assault would clear his mind— or at least wake him up.

But as he pulled back inside and slammed the window, nothing seemed to have changed. Well, he was wet. But his head was still pounding, and he felt like a complete fool. He had no better idea than before of how he'd lost his pajamas, but he felt very sure he had bigger problems at the moment than a pair of wayward pants.

Frowning, he ran his hands through his dripping hair. Could Saskia possibly be telling the truth? And if she was, what kind of lunatic did that make him, pulling strange women into his bed, whispering even stranger endearments and not remembering any of it?

"It was all a dream," he told himself resolutely. "Like sleepwalking."

And if, under the spell of some weird phantoms of the night, he'd behaved in a way that was completely foreign to him, well, he could hardly be held responsible.

But as Connor paced his red-and-black monstrosity of a room, trying to figure out what had taken place within the past few hours, he was not comforted.

Something had definitely happened here tonight, something that had fanned the flames between him and Saskia. The longer he paced, the more the memories surfaced, in vague, wispy little fragments. He had no idea what was real and what was fantasy, but he suddenly knew a lot about Saskia.

He knew how sweet her mouth tasted under his, and how soft her cheek felt against his fingers.

He remembered the curve of her hip filling his hand, and the way she wiggled and moaned when she was excited.

"Lord," he whispered, raking a hand through his hair. "This is outrageous."

But it was all mixed up with flashes of something else, of someone else. Definitely like Saskia, very like, but not quite the same. Dark, soft hair, spilling over ivory shoulders. Wide, dark eyes.

His hands clenched into fists, as anger, jealousy, rage, uncertainty and overpowering desire suddenly pumped through his veins.

He was furious. He was righteously indignant. He was a man, by God, and he'd have satisfaction if it was the last thing he ever did.

"Damn it," he roared. "You will marry me, if I have to carry you to the altar bound and gagged. You *are* the right woman for me. Society and its rules be damned!''

And then he caught himself. Astonished, he glanced down at his hand, uncurling his fingers slowly, as if he weren't quite sure how he'd gotten a fist in the first place.

What was this all about? Unsteadily, he walked into the bathroom, staring at his reflection in the mirror. Yes, it was definitely him. Wet and disheveled, but definitely Connor Wynn.

Yet if he hadn't heard the words come out of his own mouth, hadn't seen his own fingers wrapped into a ball, he would've sworn some other man had spoken.

''I'm losing my mind,'' he muttered to his image in the mirror. ''Completely and positively losing my mind.''

It was time to think rationally, if that was still possible. He splashed cold water in his face, combed his hair, got a drink, made the bed, plumped up the pillows and set up the fan Saskia had left in the hall.

And then Connor sat on the bed in his pajama bottoms, letting the air from the fan blow over his heat-glazed body. He tried as hard as he could to come up with some sort of reasonable explanation for his own behavior.

Did he have a split personality that was suddenly asserting itself?

He sincerely doubted it. He was as sane as it got, with a perfectly happy childhood behind him. Whole clusters of his classmates at prep school had been in analysis, dealing with the demons of remote parents and too much wealth. But not Connor.

So what if his mother was a slave to fashion, his father was as rich as Croesus and his sisters were poster girls for country-club snobbery? He was still the most sensible, least delusional person he knew.

Second choice: Wynnwood was haunted, with this mess the result of some ghostly escapade, some trick from the Great Beyond, all sparked by Madame Renata and her séance.

"Absolutely not," he said out loud. The whole idea was nonsense. For one thing, he didn't believe in ghosts, and certainly not at a Wynn family home.

They wouldn't dare.

Besides, that medium was as fake as a three-dollar bill and she couldn't have stirred up a spirit with a spoon.

But what about the power of suggestion? Now there was a thought.

After all, he was physically exhausted and emotionally spent after the long drive through the storm and the confrontation in the parlor. So what better time for a bunch of con artists to befuddle him enough that his unconscious mind would create a nightmare?

They'd rattled at him about ghosts and curses and spectral manifestations until he was susceptible, and then they'd stuck him in this horrible room. They were probably using him as a test case, to try out their plans to sucker paying guests. And that probably explained his weird reaction to Saskia when they first met, too. It was all part of some crackpot sorcerer's package deal. For all he knew, there were tape recorders concealed in the walls, whispering strange words in his ear as soon as he dropped off.

And once he was good and hooked, Saskia showed up, adding to the fantasy, keeping him firmly in the clutches of this manufactured ghost story.

"Now that makes a lot more sense." He settled back into the bedclothes, feeling satisfied that he had found an answer he could live with.

Well, he'd show them. In the bright light of morning, they would find out that it wasn't quite so easy to fool Connor Wynn. They could throw any number of spooky noises and beautiful women at him, and he would still see through their flimsy schemes.

He yawned, slumping down just a little into his pillows. God, he was tired. He really didn't want to fall asleep again if it meant more tricks from the Truelove women, but what else could they do now? Surely they were through for the night.

"Aw, who cares? They've hit me with their worst, and it didn't work. Do you hear that, Petunia and Primrose?" he called up into the nearest air vent. "Do you hear that, Saskia? It didn't work."

Sprawling full length on top of those ghastly red sheets, Connor closed his eyes. Just a few winks. Then he'd be ready for the next round.

Just a few... He yawned and settled into the pillows. A few winks...

DELIGHTFUL.

She smelled delightful, like spring flowers, and he always knew she'd entered the room before she said a word.

He was in his bedchamber, with the full light of the late afternoon sun beaming through the lace curtains at his window. He sat at his dressing table, fastening his cravat before a gilt-edged mirror. Behind the table, he noticed the wallpaper, patterned in dark, masculine greens and browns.

This was his room—the master's chamber. Yet he felt slightly uneasy, as if he might have expected it to look different. The armoire was where it should be, and the bed . . .

But the bed seemed to have shrunk, as if the posts had once been thicker, taller. And he had this strange feeling that the walls should be a different color.

Red and black? Wasn't this room supposed to be red and black?

But, no, of course not. He had picked out this bed, this table, this wallpaper himself. He had chosen every glass doorknob, every piece of plaster molding, so that his new home would be perfect for the woman he hoped to make his bride.

And then she swept in behind him, and he forgot his unease. She laughed gaily, setting her small hands over his eyes, and her taffeta-and-lace dress rustled provocatively as she moved in closer.

"My darling," she whispered, and the familiar surge of possessiveness, of fierce love and jealousy filled him.

"Isabelle..." he said softly, and he pulled her down across his lap.

The sweet tinkle of her laughter danced in the air, filling his ears, filling the room, and he kissed her long and hard. "You will marry me." It was an order, and no mere proposal.

"Darling, you can be so very tiresome," she complained prettily. She tried to kiss him, to steer them both away from this unpleasant subject, but he would have none of it.

"Isabelle, no more of this," he said, catching at her clever little hands. "I am an honorable man, and I want to make you my wife."

"But I am not an honorable woman." She jumped up and stalked to the window, pretending to stare out into the soft island twilight. "And that is precisely the problem. I wear trousers and smoke cigarettes in public, I take tea alone with unmarried men, and I am rumored to have shared a bed with most of the eligible men in New York. My entire life has been a scandal."

He began to interrupt, but she held her chin high in that imperious manner of hers, and her eyes flashed fire when she turned back to speak directly to him.

"I have done nothing wrong, and I refuse," she said angrily, "I simply *refuse* to be bound by the ridiculous conventions of which your pompous friends and their odious wives are so overweeningly fond."

"But, Isabelle—"

"No, darling. Please, not again. We have discussed this idiotic proposal of yours so many times that it now gives me a dreadful headache to even hear the word 'marriage.' We have nothing left to say on that subject." Her expression softened and she slid back into his lap, cradling his face with her hands. "I will come to you, only you, wherever you are." Her smile was delicious. "I will make love to you as frequently as possible. But I will not marry you."

"We cannot go on like this," he whispered, but she laughed again and ever so softly said something very naughty in his ear, and he felt himself weaken, as he always did. He could never resist her for long. She was enchanting.

Isabelle loosened his tie and his wing collar, tossing both aside. "And now we've quarreled again, and our precious moments have flown. You're expected at the Vanderbilt party tonight, aren't you, my love? I hesitate to keep you from your respectable society friends," she said dryly.

But he cared not one whit if he missed the whole affair, and she knew it. He ripped impatiently at the silk-covered buttons on her dress.

"But they're expecting you."

"I will see the Vanderbilts another day," he responded forcefully, deciding then and there that he would disrobe her and make love to her right there, on the floor in front of the dressing table.

Perhaps she would find it shocking. He smiled, enjoying the idea of shocking Isabelle, who thought herself so sophisticated.

Perhaps if he shocked her, she would see the danger and excitement lying just under the surface of her lover. Perhaps then she would learn that he was not the stodgy, puffed-up gentleman she accused him of being.

Surely then she would admit that marriage between them was the only possible choice, and not simply a surrender to the mores of a society she hated.

He was mad for her, crazy for her love, and he could not control the wild desire pushing him to make love to her again and again until she understood the power of his need and his desire, until she agreed once and for all to become his wife.

"Isabelle," he murmured, pushing her down to the floor, disposing of the layers of her clothing, until she lay naked and beautiful before him. "Isabelle..."

CONNOR AWOKE WITH A START, gripping a fistful of sheet so tightly he could barely pry his fingers apart. He sat up and looked around, but it didn't change the way he felt.

He was stunned. He was in agony. He was on fire.

On fire for Isabelle. Except she wasn't Isabelle. He might be disoriented, but he remembered that much. Her hair, her eyes, her smile, the way she held her chin... They were all so familiar he could've sketched them with his eyes closed.

He'd just been making wild, vivid, passionate, wonderful love in his dreams. To a woman who looked exactly like Saskia Truelove.

SASKIA AWOKE WITH A START. She sat up in her bed, pulling the cool linen sheet up to her chin.

"Oh, my God!" she said out loud. But she was still trembling.

She'd just been making wild, vivid, wonderful, passionate love in her dreams. To Connor Wynn.

And the whole time, he'd called her Isabelle.

Who the hell was Isabelle?

Chapter Six

Like a frightened rabbit, Saskia was hiding out.

Luckily, there were plenty of places in Wynnwood where she could go to ground, counting on the fact that no one would stumble across her.

It was ridiculous to feel this nervous, this crazed, in her own house, but she just couldn't face Connor this morning. Not after last night. Not after what they'd shared.

She closed her eyes. No matter how many doors she hid behind, no matter how many nooks and crannies she took cover in, it didn't keep him away from her. In her mind, she was still back in that bed, still dreaming of his hard bronzed body and the sinful way he . . .

"This has got to stop!" she told herself fiercely. She flicked her feather duster so hard she almost knocked the head off a porcelain bunny. "Chill out, Saskia."

After all, it was all in her mind. The poor man had no idea she'd been fantasizing about him. Although she felt sure he could take one look at her flushed face and wide, expectant eyes and figure it out. Which was why she had not sought him out first thing this morning, even though that was the agreement they'd made last night.

No, she'd played hide-and-seek instead, instructing her aunts to tell Connor she was busy and would try to talk to him later, whenever she got a free moment. And then she'd dug up some very remote tasks to occupy herself with, like dusting the knickknacks in the north-wing sitting room, which you could only get to if you used three different staircases and walked in a circle for ten minutes.

Even way up here, she kept thinking she heard his step in the hall, or his voice outside her door. She jumped every time a floorboard creaked, which was plenty often in this place. Until finally there were no more Wedgwood candy dishes and Chinese vases left to dust.

"Time to stop being such a coward," she told herself. Besides, it was well past time for lunch, and she was starving. Hunger came before cowardice on her priority list.

Cautiously, Saskia slipped out of the sitting room. No one around. That was a relief.

"This is all my aunts' fault," she griped, as she snaked her way down the hall like Mata Hari. "If it weren't for them and their stupid love potion, neither Connor nor I would be drowning in this bizarre sea of sticky desire. And then I wouldn't be afraid to face Connor, and I could lead a normal life again." She paused. "Face it, Saskia, you never did lead a normal life."

And then it hit her. If they could chant a few bad rhymes and catch her in this impossible tangle...then there must be an equally bad rhyme to make it go away.

"I'll just insist they chant it backward or something," she said, still riding this burst of inspiration. But the spark died as quickly as it had come. "They'd never do it. And even if I could get them to agree to try, they'd screw it up, just like they did this time."

She was still a little miffed about the Isabelle thing. It was one thing to ensnare a guy with a goofy love potion. But it was quite another to have him fall into the trap like a ripe plum and then call her by the wrong name! If this was supposed to fulfill her fantasies, it was sorely lacking.

She had no idea how the name Isabelle figured into this equation, but from long experience with the Truelove brand of witchery her best guess was that her aunts had botched some portion of the spell, big time. But asking them to retrace their steps and excise Isabelle was like telling Dracula he'd missed the vein and offering him another crack at your neck.

In other words, it was asking for trouble.

"But if they can't take away the spell," she murmured, "maybe *I* can."

Why not? She was no witch, but then neither were her aunts. Plus she was a lot more organized and efficient than they were, and she had a much better talent for following recipes. If all it took were a few words of mumbo jumbo and stirring up a pot of goop to un-love-potion somebody, surely Saskia could do it.

She smiled. All she had to do was leaf through a book or two and find a likely sounding potion, something guaranteed to wipe out any previous spells. She could do it. She hadn't hung around with Petunia and Primrose all these years for nothing.

Deciding that time was of the essence, Saskia postponed lunch for the moment and set off in search of mystical tomes. *Grimoires*, her aunts called them. She knew her best bet would be their bedrooms, since they each kept their favorite books of magic close at hand.

After racing down a different set of stairs to the second floor, she crept silently out into the west hallway where her aunts' bedrooms were situated. She was gliding along, doing fine, until she heard approaching voices.

And one of them was male.

She backed into a vacant bedroom, peeking out through a crack, just as Connor and Aunt Petunia went marching by.

"She's here somewhere, and I know she's anxious to get this settled," Petunia announced. She had Connor by the hand and she was literally towing him down the hall. "Now, why are you dragging your feet, young man?"

"I'm not," he swore, but even Saskia could see he was.

My, my, my, but he looked good. Just like in her dream. Except he was wearing clothes this time, of course. She wondered idly if he really had that intriguing birthmark on his thigh.

No, of course he didn't. It was just a silly, made-up dream, with silly, made-up birthmarks and silly, made-up thighs. Although even in her imagination, she'd never thought up rock-hard, sinewy thighs such as his.

Saskia blushed hotly, all by herself in the empty bedroom.

"Why don't you want to see Saskia?" Petunia demanded. "She's miles too good for the likes of you, Commodore, so you needn't be snobby."

"I'm not being snobby. I just had other things to take care of this morning."

So he wasn't in any greater hurry to run into her than she was to run into him. Maybe he was embarrassed he'd pulled her into his bed so rudely and talked to her so strangely. Come to think of it, he'd talked like that in the dream, too. She'd almost forgotten about the *real* intimacies they'd shared in the wake of the much more intimate dream.

But for whatever reason, he seemed as anxious to avoid her as she was to avoid him, even though Petunia was doing her best to effect a meeting. Leave it to Petunia.

"Come along then," her aunt said huffily, grabbing his arm in a very peremptory manner. "We haven't got all day. I know Saskia must be up here somewhere. She had the feather duster in her hand when she left, and she only uses that on the bookcases in the library, the paintings in the south gallery and the porcelains in the north sitting room. We've tried the other two, so it must be the porcelains. Hurry it up, Mr. Wynn, or we'll miss her!"

"And wouldn't that be a shame," Connor muttered.

Saskia only heard him because he happened to be inches from her door when he said it. She ducked farther back, her pulse pounding. Too close!

But Petunia just kept on chugging, steering him down the hall and then up the winding staircase that led eventually to the sitting room. Their voices receded into more remote corners of Wynnwood.

Saskia leaned against the inside of the door, drained. Good grief! If this was how she felt after just a glimpse, how would she feel if she'd had to speak to him?

She wiped a shaky hand across her forehead. Aunt Petunia was pretty crafty, and they hadn't missed her by much.

But there was no time to worry about that now. Seeing him up close had only intensified her feeling that she must find a way to counteract the love spell. Otherwise, she'd be doomed to stand around drooling over him at every possible moment.

Okay, so it was insane to go boiling things in cauldrons in the faint hope that she could undo her aunts' mischief. But at least it was unlikely to make things any worse. Wasn't it?

"Desperate times, desperate measures," she said under her breath, letting herself into Petunia's bedroom.

As she'd hoped, there were books all over. Several of them had fancy gold scrolling across the front, one featuring a big, black cat not unlike Banquo, and two had borders of Egyptian hieroglyphs. Where to begin?

She immediately discarded anything not in English, since she knew no Latin whatsoever and had only a smattering of Italian and French from cooking classes. That wasn't nearly enough to decipher and eliminate ancient recipes for curing three-legged calves, or setting the evil eye on unfriendly neighbors. With her luck, she'd sneeze on the wrong page and set a horde of gremlins loose under Aunt Petunia's bed.

"Knowing her, she would probably be thrilled," Saskia muttered.

At last, she had her hands on a fat, trustworthy-looking book, completely in English, called *The Good Witch's Guide to Life*. It had nice, modern topics, such as "Wreathmaking to Celebrate Lammas," whatever Lammas was, and "Stabilizing Household Spirits with Tea." Sounded good.

But as she frantically thumbed through the index, looking for anything on love spells or how to reverse them, she thought she heard noises outside in the corridor.

Voices. Footsteps.

Someone was coming. And then she heard the tell-tale rattle of the doorknob. Without thinking, with *The Good Witch's Guide* still in her hand, Saskia ran for the closet.

She left the door open just a bit, so she could hear whoever it was, as she edged back behind Petunia's bathrobe and rack of lavender-scented dresses for cover.

"I have just the thing right here," Aunt Primrose said loudly from the main room. "I know Petunia had it out just the other day, and she was reading to me all about brewing tea to calm restless ghosts. Just what the Commodore needs, don't you think?"

Saskia glanced down at the book in her hand. "Stabilizing Household Spirits with Tea" was Chapter Four. She was holding the book Primrose was looking for.

"I agree completely. I think some kind of balancing spell is exactly what we need," Madame Renata intoned. Dramatically, her voice rose when she said, "Ever since the séance, I've felt the presence of a spirit—a strong, restless, unhappy spirit. I am convinced we are being haunted. We are being haunted by the Commodore, and now we must soothe his fevered soul."

"We don't want to send him back, though," Primrose returned tartly. "Just calm him down a bit." Her voice dropped, and Saskia heard the shuffling of volumes and pages. "Now where can that book have gotten to? Look on the dresser, will you, Madame? I'll see if it's in on the shelf in the closet."

Yikes. Primrose was headed straight for her!

She tried to crouch farther back, but her hand on the book was sweaty, and for just a second she lost her grip. She scrabbled for it, trying to catch it without making any noise, but all she succeeded in doing was letting the book slip through her fingers and completely losing her balance.

Dresses and hangers careened madly, the book clattered to the floor and Saskia took a step back, right on top of a pile of Aunt Petunia's favorite high-heeled pumps. Her foot shot out from under her, her hands flew out to try to find some kind of brace and she fully expected to find herself flat on her rump, staring up at Primrose's shocked face.

But her bottom never hit the floor. Instead, the back of the closet gave way against her hand, as if she'd swung open a door, and Saskia went somersaulting right out of the closet, with two pairs of pumps and *The Good Witch's Guide to Life* sailing along for the ride.

Above her, she could hear the disembodied voice of Aunt Primrose call out, "There's nothing in here now. It must have been the Commodore's ghost, trying to scare us!"

But Saskia could do little more than whimper as she went scuttling down, rolling and tumbling, down into the great, slippery black chute that had sucked her right out of Aunt Petunia's closet.

CONNOR TIPTOED INTO the library, relieved to find no one there. It had been a lot easier than he'd thought to steer clear of Saskia, although her aunts were another matter. He would no sooner dodge one than the other one would come running.

"Don't you want to see Saskia?" they kept asking, inventing reasons why he needed to go head-to-head with their beauteous niece.

No, I don't want to see Saskia, he felt like shouting. *Not while I'm this confused.*

Dreams of Saskia, dreams of Isabelle who *was* Saskia, Isabelle's bronzes—he wasn't confused, he was coming unhinged.

He seriously considered digging his car out of the mud pit it was in, driving away and never coming back. But how could he do that? How could he leave Wynnwood with so much unexplained?

"You met a pretty girl and you had a hot dream about her—nothing so strange there," he told himself. "And you were already wondering about Isabelle, because of the missing statues, so you just stuck her name on Saskia in your subconscious. Nothing so weird there, either."

In an effort to make himself believe that, he was going to try to find out some more information about the Commodore and his art collections. He dearly hoped that solving the mystery of the statues—who Isabelle was or at least why the statues were named after her—would free his brain from some of its current strain.

"Isabelle was probably the Commodore's favorite cocker spaniel," he said moodily. "I'm driving myself crazy for a bunch of cocker spaniel statues. I was obviously overworked and I needed a vacation, or I wouldn't have gotten so excited by the idea of some missing bronzes in the first place."

Once he was convinced that the bronzes were just another dusty piece of mediocre artwork, Isabelle would cease to be a mystery, the dreams would vanish and he could leave Wynnwood in peace. And what better place to start this mission to find Isabelle than in the old man's library?

Or at least that was the theory.

Getting the lay of the huge, cavernous room, he bypassed a big rolltop desk that looked to be Saskia's center of business operations, glancing around instead at the heavy leather chairs, the long carved bookshelves and the arched windows that looked out onto the lawn. Outside, two intertwined live oak trees, the gnarled, twisted kind that trailed spanish moss, brought to mind a Southern plantation. Very atmospheric.

But inside the silent library, Connor felt completely alone, with nothing but a few dust motes and a lot of books to keep him company.

"Aw, what are you worried about?" he asked himself.

But he knew exactly what he was worried about. Saskia.

He was afraid that she would come waltzing into the library, all fired up because he'd avoided her all day, and he would take one look at those luminous eyes, that impertinent little mouth, those long, slim legs ... and be unable to control his baser instincts.

Just like in the dream, he would grab her and make love to her until they were both senseless.

"What we did in that dream was unbelievable," he murmured, still half in shock.

Well, until the shock wore off, until the memory lost a little of its raw edge, he was safer not being anywhere near her.

Which brought him back to the library.

Reluctantly, he gave up his lascivious visions of Saskia and came back to earth, back to his search. Diaries or journals would've been nice—something in the Commodore's own hand that rambled on about why he was ordering a whole series of statues from a famous French artist, and who or what their subject was.

But Connor really doubted that his great-grandfather was the diary kind. From all accounts, he was a grim, brooding man, completely absorbed in his business deals, with no time to spend on annoyances such as family or pets. So much for the cocker spaniel theory.

"Okay, Commodore," Connor mused, "if not diaries, I know you're the kind of guy who would've left complete household accounts somewhere, including what you had in the house and where you stored it. And I'm hoping that includes a description of—and pinpoint location for—the elusive Isabelle bronzes." He ran his forefinger over a dusty row of books. "We've got the three-volume set of *Salt Marshes,* and six volumes on *Flora and Fauna of the Coastal Waterways.* Very nice. But where's the section on Wynnwood?"

He kept looking, methodically making his way around the library, through book after book on gardening and sailing, plus leather-bound sets of Dickens and Thackeray and Shakespeare. If the dust was any indication, this place definitely looked like no one had disturbed its contents for many years.

"Old Aunt Poppy wasn't much of a reader, I guess," he said out loud. He was relieved when no one answered him back.

Finally, at the very top of a tall bookcase, he spotted what he thought he was searching for. There they were, a set of what looked to be about thirty account books. Although the words printed on the spines were faded and difficult to read, if he squinted he thought he could make out numbers at the base of each spine. Like the individual years the accounts were from, perhaps?

Perfect. Now, if only he could reach them. Although he was tall, he wasn't a giant. The books were at about the twelve-foot mark, if he was any judge. Quickly, Connor looked around for something to stand on, sure there must be some way to get up to those journals.

"Aha," he said, as he spotted a wrought-iron ladder pushed down to the end of the shelves.

It was more ornate than necessary, with dragons and griffins fashioned into the sides to provide handholds. At the top, some sort of stylized claw curved into the bookcase; it looked like the claw fitted into a groove that ran all the way around the gallery, so that you could slide the ladder to whatever part of the library you wanted. In theory, at least.

When he actually tried to slide it, it wouldn't budge, and it made a horrible groaning noise when he tried to force it.

Since he was trying not to call attention to himself, he laid off immediately. But there was nothing else in the library to stand on, except a few leather wing chairs that weren't nearly tall enough.

With a sigh of resignation, he gave in and returned to the ladder. As soon as he touched it, it started that awful scraping, screeching noise again, but there was nothing he could do but just let it go. Since the house was so huge, he could only hope the racket he was making was confined to this room, or the Truelove ladies would be after him again.

After much pushing and shoving, Connor managed to get the ladder moving. Eventually, he got the thing lined up all the way at the end, right next to the journals he wanted to see.

Since it was so heavy, at least he was sure the thing was sturdy. In a flash, Connor mounted the ladder, reaching out for the nearest book, the one he could now see was marked "1913." Hopefully, this would tell him everything he'd ever wanted to know about the fate of the household in that year. Like how many paintings and knickknacks the Commodore had purchased, and maybe a handy inventory of the famous bronzes.

Quickly, Connor blew the dust off the top and then leaned back against the ladder to open the volume. But the first few pages were blank. That didn't make sense. He thumbed through the rest of the book, but it was the same—plain, white and empty.

Well, maybe the Commodore had never gotten around to filling in his accounts for 1913. Connor pulled out 1912. But it had the same problem—lots of white pages.

Why would anyone keep these account books, all neatly labeled with the years they were supposed to cover, if they had never even been used? "Maybe he did use them but he wrote in disappearing ink," Connor joked into the empty room. He wouldn't have put it past the old coot.

Determined to get to the bottom of the mystery, Connor reached out for 1911. But it was just beyond his grasp, and he had to lean out a little farther. To keep his balance, he grabbed onto the big iron claw that held the ladder permanently in its track.

"Whoa," he said shakily, because that maneuver hadn't steadied him at all. Instead, the claw shifted down with a clunk, almost like a lever of some kind. And then the whole ladder seemed to be rotating—noiselessly, smoothly, effortlessly—and the bookcase with it!

As he hung on for dear life, the bookcase spun into a 180° turn, wheeling him out of the bright library and into complete darkness. There was just a skinny crack of light, where the bookcase hadn't completely closed behind him.

Connor sat there, still perched at the top of his ladder, while down below what seemed to be a secret passage wound away into nowhere.

"What is this, the Hardy Boys?" he asked uneasily. His voice echoed in the narrow confines of the dark corridor.

He knew he was crazy, but he couldn't resist. Jumping down off the ladder, he felt his way along the wall, stealthily making his way into the passage.

"Whatever's in here, I'm going to find it," he said under his breath.

And on he crept, into the darkness. The walls were curving, and the passage seemed to be leading him toward the middle of the house. The floor slanted up slightly, and he wasn't surprised when he reached a narrow stairway, climbing crookedly up to another level.

As he sneaked along, he came across several small branches that led off the main passage, but he kept to the largest part, deciding that was the safest bet to stick with, since he really wasn't all that familiar with the structure of the house.

At one point there was even a small door fitted into the wall. He tried the handle, but it seemed to be locked from the other side, wedged too tightly for him to even force it. Besides, he wasn't sure his shoulders would fit through that small opening.

All he needed was to get stuck halfway through a door in the tunnel, where no one would ever find him. For the first time, he understood why secret passageways in books always had skeletons lying in them.

"Because people like me wander in and can't get out," he said grimly. His words reverberated around him, mocking him.

Gradually, the passage got smaller and darker. As the ceiling descended over his head, Connor had to crouch and to move more slowly, one hand outstretched in front of him. He couldn't see a thing.

But still he inched forward, feeling the way with his fingers, hoping that sooner or later the passage would come out somewhere.

Until it took a short dip and then curved down and around in a different direction. Suddenly, the air was cooler, less dense, and the passageway seemed to have opened up, with a higher ceiling and a bit more breathing room. He could just make out what looked like a ladder or maybe a circular staircase, dead ahead.

As he slowed up to inspect his surroundings, to see if he had any other choice besides those rickety stairs, he heard a large whooshing sound coming from up above him.

What was that, a giant bird?

But it was whimpering. He had just enough time to throw a hand in front of his face before a trapdoor above him flapped open and he was hit on the head by what felt like a shoe and then a book.

And then something huge was on top of him. He was thrown to the ground, thoroughly squashed, by a screaming, thrashing bundle of arms and legs. Around the pain and surprise of being attacked by a flying invader, he could feel . . . softness. Cotton? Denim?

Something in blue jeans was smashing into his abdomen. Silky hair flicked across his face, soft skin brushed his cheek and an elbow pressed one of his ribs almost clear through his lung.

"Oof," he said, trying to take in some air. His attacker wiggled a little, rolling to one side far enough that he could at least get a clear breath. Thank goodness.

When he breathed in, he got a strong whiff of a familiar scent: springtime. And his brain processed what the rest of his body had already known for several minutes.

Saskia.

Like an angel summarily tossed off her cloud, Saskia Truelove had come flying through the air and landed smack-dab on top of him.

Chapter Seven

"Connor," she breathed with relief. Her heart was racing, and she felt like she was probably black-and-blue from her free-fall, but she ignored it. She flattened herself on top of him and held on for dear life. "Thank God you were here to break my fall."

"Yeah, right," he said in a muffled tone, but he didn't sound any too thankful. He sounded squashed.

Still, he didn't let go, just rearranged them both a little. Supporting her securely in the circle of his arms, he sat up and cradled her against his chest.

Saskia took a moment to collect herself, to rest against him, trying to catch her breath. What in the world had just happened here? She had no idea where they were or how he'd come to be underneath her at exactly the right moment.

It was just her luck to be trying to avoid him, and then to do an Alice-in-Wonderland routine, falling out the back of her aunt's closet and right on top of him. She couldn't just bump into him in the hallway like a normal person. *Hi, how are you? Fine, thanks, and you?* No, she had to come careening out of some sort of cosmic laundry chute.

It just went to prove that there were some things she was better off not trying to avoid. Fate had a way of catching up with her.

His heartbeat was as erratic as her own, and she realized she'd probably scared him as badly as she had scared herself. But she could worry about that later. Right now, she was in a state of shock, and the best therapy seemed to be to wind her arms around Connor's neck and hold on tight.

Too late, she remembered that this was exactly why she was avoiding him in the first place. She'd been afraid they'd end up in this position. Well, too bad. It wasn't every day you fell out of a closet into never-never land. You took your comfort where you got it. Even if it was very risky comfort.

"Are you, um, all right?" he asked unsteadily.

"Yes, I think so. You?"

He seemed fine to her, with everything exactly where it should be. Up close and personal, she was pressed against him, her breasts brushing his chest, one thigh rubbing the hard ridge of his hip. *Oh, yes.* Everything was exactly where it was supposed to be.

"Anything broken?" he asked gruffly, as his fingers probed gently around her arms and her waist, over her ribs, up a little higher...

Somehow, she didn't think it was too likely that anything was going to be broken in the areas he was currently checking out so thoroughly, but she wasn't complaining.

His eyes were so blue, so amazing, even in this dim light. Saskia licked her lips. The expression in Connor's eyes was ardent and hungry, exactly as she'd imagined it would be.

And then he unexpectedly kissed her on the neck, lingering for a long beat.

"Oh, my," she whispered. She closed her eyes and slid forward, closer into his embrace, rubbing her cheek on his, making little moaning sounds like a hungry kitten.

In fact, she was acting as shamelessly as he was. And she didn't care.

One hard arm encircled her waist as his other hand skirted the edge of her cotton shirt, tugging it out where it was tucked into her jeans. His clever fingers slipped under the fabric, and then they were cool and tingly against her fevered skin, sliding up, just brushing the underside of her breast.

"Oh, yes," she murmured, as he suddenly picked up his pace, swiftly undoing her buttons, dropping soft, sweet kisses along the line of skin he uncovered as each button slipped free of its silken sheath.

Intent on his task, he lifted his head to nip at her lips, greedily kissing her and touching her, using enough potent force to knock them both over backward, back to the floor.

"You know this is crazy, don't you?" she said, raggedly trying to breathe, but her hands were already ripping at his buttons and pushing away his shirt.

"I know, but I don't care." His jaw clenched, and he held his body in rigid check, waiting for her reaction.

"Neither do I," she said fervently, and then she angled a hand around the back of his neck, to maneuver him closer.

He kissed her again, harder this time, delving into her mouth with wet, warm, demanding strokes, and she responded in kind. Her head was spinning and she could hardly breathe, but she didn't give up, didn't pull away. It was crazy, but it was what they both wanted, what they both needed, more than anything in the world.

He pressed his body urgently, impatiently, against hers, making his heavy desire clear. Saskia tried to roll with him, to melt into the source of all that heat, but she was a little too eager. Her foot got trapped between him and the floorboard, and she yelped with sudden, intense, shooting pain.

As she cried out, Connor jumped back, clearly horrified that he had hurt her. He hit the smooth plaster wall of the tunnel behind them with a thump, and then he seemed to simply disappear.

She saw the outline of a gaping black hole for about half a second, and then the plaster slid soundlessly, smoothly back into place, as if it had never moved at all.

"Connor?" she shouted.

She scooted over there, pounding on the wall with all her might. She was terrified that she had lost him. Or maybe he'd never been there in the first place, and she'd been making love with a phantom again.

At Wynnwood, anything was possible.

"Connor!" She hit her fist hard on the wall, just where she thought she'd seen him last. "Where did you go?"

"I'm here," he called out faintly. His voice seemed to be coming from below her, but she was too happy to hear it to quibble. "Can you hear me?"

"Yes, yes! Thank God." Slumping against the plaster with relief, Saskia accidentally sat down on her foot and let out an anguished "yeow" all over again.

"Are you okay? What was that?" he demanded. The whole wall vibrated as Connor pounded on it from the other side.

"I'm fine. It was my stupid ankle again. I must have twisted it when I fell the first time, and then just not noticed...for a while," she finished lamely. She'd been too busy with other things to discover a mere twisted ankle.

With her hands flat against the plaster, she leaned down to the bottom and asked slowly, with careful enunciation, "Where are you? What happened?"

"My shoulder hit the wall, and it was just like a door swung open behind me. I slid down a short ramp, right into a room of some sort. I can't quite get back up to where you are, but I can hear you just fine."

"Just like Aunt Petunia's closet," she told him. "I fell out the back, right into a tunnel."

"What were you doing in Aunt Petunia's closet?"

"I'll tell you later. Can you get out of there? Or can I come in?"

"I'm working on it. Just stay put for a second, okay?" His voice floated around in a different direction, and she imagined him surveying his surroundings over there. "I know there must be a mechanism here somewhere. But I can't even find a crack."

But there was no way she was staying put, all alone in a dark tunnel with a sprained ankle. The chances of werewolves or vampires creeping up on her seemed very remote, but Saskia wasn't planning on sitting still long enough to play those odds.

If Connor had hit the right spot and found the door, then so could she. After hurriedly buttoning up her blouse, just in case any monsters happened by while she was looking for an escape route, she picked up one of Aunt Petunia's high heels, which had rolled over into the corner, and tapped the shoe all along the wall. One spot in particular seemed to make a hollow thud when she hit it, rather than the clink she got elsewhere.

On one foot, gingerly, Saskia rammed her shoulder at the sweet spot. Nothing. She rammed it again, with everything she had, and she heard the right sort of dull thunk.

And then she slipped, and went tumbling down into nowhere.

For the second time, Connor caught her at the bottom. At least this time he seemed to be prepared, if she was judging from the neat way he snagged her.

"Thanks again for breaking my fall," she said lightly.

She noted idly that he had refastened his shirt, too, but he hadn't matched the buttons up right. The desperate mood of the encounter outside seemed to have passed, but she still found herself wishing she could rip off that shirt and start all over.

"I thought I told you to stay put," he returned, pulling her to her feet, but he gave her a quick hug that was so fierce she didn't think he could be too angry. "Now we're both trapped in here."

"You mean there's no way out?" she asked with a sinking heart. Trapped in a secret room with Connor Wynn. Well, she could think of worse fates.

"I haven't found one yet, but there must be a way to get back out the way we came in. Let's hope it doesn't only open from the outside," he said grimly.

"Better that we should both be trapped in the same place than one of us in here and the other one out there," Saskia put in, trying to brace herself against him so she didn't have to stand on her ankle, which was really killing her now.

"But you weren't trapped out there." He swung her up into his arms, taking her a few steps farther into the room, where he carefully deposited her in a small overstuffed chair. As he bent to take a closer look at her ankle, he told her, "All you would've had to do was follow the secret passageway, and you would've ended up back down in the library."

"You came in through the library?"

"Yeah." But his attention was focused on her foot. He removed her sneaker and then propped her foot in the palm of his hand, holding it as cautiously as if it was made of glass, as he flexed it back and forth a little at a time. "It doesn't look too bad. You probably just twisted it."

"I know," she said, trying to wrest it away from him without causing herself too much pain. Oh, well. Might as well let him hang onto her foot for a few minutes, if he really wanted to. It was a pleasant feeling, wiggling her toes in the palm of his hand. "So what happened in the library?"

"A section of shelves completely spun around, and took me with them." He grinned, and she was swept away by the sheer, devilish charm of that smile. "Just like Batman," he said mischievously, "except there was no pole down to the Bat Cave. Or not one that I discovered, anyway."

"This is incredible. You walked through a bookcase and I take a big fall out of the back of Aunt Petunia's closet, and at exactly the same time. What are the chances of that happening?" Saskia just sat there, utterly astonished, trying not to wince with pain every time he shifted her foot around. "It's like this place has a mind of its mind, not to mention a whole infestation of trapdoors and tunnels. It's like living in the fun house at the fair."

"And you didn't know about any of these secret passages before?"

She flashed him a wary look. "No, of course not. What did you think, this was all part of my ghostbuster plot?"

"Well, it was a possibility," he said stiffly.

"I can assure you this is the first I've heard of it. Who would've guessed?" She shook her head. "Well, actually, we probably should've guessed, as strange as this house is, that it was hiding secrets somewhere. So the Commodore built in a whole network of secret tunnels and passageways, hmm? What a guy."

"And rooms," Connor said, setting her foot down and looking around thoughtfully. "Or at least one secret room. This one."

"I hadn't thought of that." Eyes wide, she boosted herself up on the arms of her chair, trying to shift around far enough to give the place a quick once-over.

She wasn't sure she'd ever been in a perfectly round room before, and this one was especially odd, since it had absolutely no doors. If she hadn't slid down that ramp herself, she'd have thought the wall was slanted on that side for no reason, and that the only way in or out was the window.

It was a tall, skinny window, made of clear leaded glass, slicing the outside wall like a clerestory window in a medieval castle. Not much light came through, because of the angle and the narrowness of the window, she expected. But the round room didn't seem to be dark or gloomy, even with its lack of light. In fact, it was very charming.

Other than the window, the room had no features, really, and very little furniture. There was the comfy chair Connor had set her down on, and a matching red velvet sofa, plus a small curved fireplace, and a few built-in cases haphazardly filled with books and the scattered pieces of a chess game. Several tasseled pillows lay on a small Oriental rug in the center of the hardwood floor.

She couldn't have explained it, even to herself, but she immediately liked this room. It conjured up childhood feelings, of treehouses and decoder rings, of playing Storm the Castle with her special friends.

It had all the markings, in fact, of a terrific playroom.

"Isn't this place great?" she enthused. Hobbling past Connor, she crossed to the window and peered out. She could just make out a corner of the garden, perhaps a few rosebushes. "We're on the north side, three floors up, I think. We must be in the tower. The tower room, like Rapunzel!"

She laughed and tried to spin around, but it was tough with only one good leg. "Isn't this fantastic? You know, I remember seeing this window from outside. I wondered what it was. I thought it looked like the kind of slot the castle guards used to shoot their arrows out of."

"Not here, they didn't," he said close behind her. "Robin Hood was a bit before my great-grandfather's time."

"Of course. I just meant it was the right spirit, if not the right historical period," she said with exasperation.

Why was he raining on her parade? Didn't he like the room as well as she did?

But she couldn't tell by looking at him. Connor was wearing a funny, moody expression, one that was hard to read. His hands were jammed into the pockets of his khaki pants, and he appeared to be gritting his teeth. She took this to mean he was either grouchy or trying hard to control himself.

Given the embrace they'd shared out on the floor of the passage, she figured it was the latter. Now that he'd had a moment to reflect, he was trying to play the gentleman. Except it seemed pretty obvious that part of him didn't want to play the gentleman.

Join the crowd. Part of her didn't want him to, either.

But she told herself that he was right, that they had become carried away by a very strange situation, and that it wouldn't, couldn't happen again. They had been playing right into her aunts' hands, and Saskia had too much of a sense of her own personal honor to be a party to that kind of trickery. She was also too stubborn and too independent to want to do things her aunts' way.

Now that they weren't plastered all over each other, now that they had to look at each other and think up some kind of rational conversation, it was quite awkward all around.

Balancing on one foot, she hopped over to the red velvet sofa, where she sat down with a great sploosh of ancient dust. "Comfortable," she said, trying to act chipper and pretend that what had happened when she fell on top of him had never happened.

This also required blocking out the previous night's scenes, including both the real one in his bed, and the fantasy one in her dreams. It took a lot of effort to remain calm with all that exposed flesh jumping around in her head.

"So, do you think this was a playroom? For the Commodore's kids?"

"A playroom?" he asked, with a sardonic tilt of one bronze eyebrow. "Not for kids, anyway."

"What do you mean?"

"I think this was quite clearly a love nest."

"A love nest?" She felt hot color creep up into her cheeks. This blushing stuff was becoming a habit when she was around Connor. "Why would you think that?"

He shrugged. "The velvet sofa, the pillows on the floor, the lack of lighting. Not to mention all the tiny naked ladies carved into the marble on that fireplace."

He would notice *that*. She certainly hadn't.

His eyes seemed to darken, and his gaze grew more intense. "The remote location is also a clue. Here, they could make as much noise as they wanted to, safely out of range of the servants' ears."

She was dying a slow and painful death, while her overworked imagination conjured up the kinds of erotic, seductive sounds a pair of lovers might make when they were all alone in their special secret room. Connor was a full ten feet away, but his words were close enough to tantalize her, to scandalize her, to make her wonder what kind of noises *he* made in the throes of passion.

"And then there's the fact that there's nothing to do up here except make love," he added lazily.

"W-what about the chessboard?"

"I figure," he said softly, "that was for after." He bent to pick up a carved ivory knight lying near the edge of the rug, and he rolled it back and forth between his long, elegant fingers. "They would lie on the pillows, drink a glass of wine perhaps, and play a game or two of chess, until they were ready for round two."

Good heavens. Round two? What did that mean?

"This is all circumstantial evidence," she said bravely. "It could just as easily have been the playroom for the Commodore's children."

"No, it couldn't." Connor dropped the chess piece on the top shelf of one of the bookcases, and then he gave her a sultry, shady smile. "I have inside knowledge, you see. The Commodore never brought his children to this house. He built the house and wintered here, but only before he was married. After he acquired the wife and kids, he never came back."

"But that's terrible! Wynnwood is a wonderful house. Why wouldn't he share it with his family?"

"Too busy forging an empire, I guess." He ambled a bit closer. "How's your ankle?"

"Fine. Well, the same." She edged backward on the sofa, not really trusting herself to sit too near him. He seemed to have taken a severe mood shift in the last few moments, and now he was acting all sexy and predatory. All he needed was a silk smoking jacket and a snifter of brandy to pop right into the previous night's dream.

She wasn't sure she liked this tendency of his to split into different personalities at the drop of a hat.

"You look a little flushed, Saskia," he said softly, sidling right up next to her and pulling her foot into his lap.

As he began to rub his thumb idly along her instep, she realized something. He might be acting like the man in the dream, but he'd gotten her name right this time.

Somehow, that made it even worse. With one shoe off and one shoe on, she ducked out from under him and hopped over to the little white fireplace opposite.

"Now isn't this charming?" she asked, leaning against the carved marble mantel for balance.

She had forgotten the thing was full of naked ladies, however, and she accidentally grabbed one right on the breast.

"Oops," she said hastily, trying to put her hand on something else. But the second one her hand landed on made a lurching noise and began to give way.

As she stared down at it in horror, the whole marble figure started to pull out of the mantel. As the cold, perky nude quivered there in midair, Connor said, "That's just what happened to me with a dragon's claw in the library. Maybe it opens another door."

But as he came running over, eager to look for exits, Saskia heard the click of shifting gears, coming from inside the chimney of the fireplace. And suddenly a large painting dropped into place from out of nowhere. It hovered there over the fireplace, serene and silent, as if it had always been there.

Buzzing with excitement, Saskia got up on tiptoe to examine this curious portrait. It was a lovely work, a large, dark oil painting of a young woman. She was seated, leaning well forward on her chair and clutching a small bouquet of flowers in one hand. Her eyes were wide and expressive, and her dark curls were swept up into a Gibson Girl hairdo. Several ropes of pearls circled her slender neck, above the rather elaborate flounces on her low, square neckline.

There was mischief in her eyes and a great deal of character stamped on her proud features.

"Well, that's strange. She looks kind of like me, don't you think?" Saskia ventured.

"That chin," he whispered. "It's you exactly."

She began to get a very funny feeling about this, deep in the pit of her stomach. Tiny stars danced in the periphery of her vision. As she squinted to read the script on a small brass plate screwed into the frame, she heard Connor mumble something behind her.

"Isabelle," he said, with a definite sense of dread, just as she read that very name off the brass plate.

"Isabelle?" she echoed, aghast.

More hopefully, Connor added, "She's not a cocker spaniel."

"A cocker spaniel? Of course not! I could've told you she was no dog."

He sent her a swift glance. "How do you know?"

"She was in my dream last night," she blurted, before she had a chance to think better of it. "I-I mean, she wasn't there, exactly, but I was. And you kept calling me by her name."

"I called you Isabelle," he repeated.

"Yes. It was really annoying, actually. Not at the time, I mean. During the dream, it was perfectly natural that you called me Isabelle, but after, it seemed a little odd. I wondered who she was, and why you called me that, but now that I see the resemblance, I guess it makes sense. I guess." She tipped her head to one side. "Well, not really, does it?"

But she could tell by the dazed look on his face that she had said too much.

He asked slowly, "Do you mean you had that dream, too?"

Saskia felt her mouth fall open. "Are you saying *you* did?" she demanded, in a voice that was at least an octave higher than her normal one. "But if you had the same dream, then you already know that we were... that we were..."

"Oh, yeah, I know," he muttered, in a rough, husky tone that left no doubt about how much he knew.

"Oh, my God! You know!"

She started to back away from him, but there was nowhere to go. Saskia was trapped.

Trapped in a secret love nest with the phantom lover of the steamiest dream she'd ever had.

Chapter Eight

"But how could we have exactly the same dream?" He ruffled his hair with a shaky hand. "That's not possible. It's like a hypnotic suggestion or something. But when were we hypnotized? No, it's not possible."

It was the stupid love potion, of course. She'd already suspected it was behind *her* dream, but she hadn't thought far enough ahead to realize a spell was capable of scorching more than one person simultaneously with its uncontrollable passion flames.

But what kept echoing in her brain now was: *Oh, God! He knows about the dream! He knows what I did, and what he did, and how incredibly good it felt, and...*

"One of these things has to work," she cried suddenly, grasping for every breast and thigh on the fireplace. Finally, one particularly busty carving slid upside down when she jiggled it, and a wooden ladder fell down from the ceiling.

"Couldn't the Commodore just have built doors like everybody else?" she groaned, despairing as she looking up at the spindly thing. It seemed to be attached to a square opening in the ceiling. It was an escape hatch, but not much of one.

"There's no way you're scaling that with a twisted ankle," Connor announced. "You'll fall and kill yourself. And you don't even know where it goes."

But she finished tying her shoe with a flourish. "I don't care—I'm getting out of here." Taking a deep breath, she set her good foot on the ladder and started to climb. It wasn't so hard if she held on very tight, and sort of hopped a little at a time.

"Saskia," he called from down below. "There has to be some rational explanation for this. We can figure it out. Don't go running off, please?"

I already know the explanation, and it isn't rational in the least. What was she supposed to say? *Oh, by the way, my aunts brewed up this concoction in the attic, and now you and I are having dreams right out of the* Kama Sutra, *and somehow some dearly departed lady who looks just like me is also involved.* Right. That would convince him.

No, she wasn't sticking around, and she wasn't offering ridiculous explanations. She was going to get back into the house's network of secret passages, hopefully right to the spot where she'd first fallen from the sky. And then she was going to retrieve her magic book and hotfoot it to the kitchen, back in the real world, where she could hopefully brew up a real humdinger of a counterspell and get them both out of this mess.

It was the best plan she could think of at the moment.

She heard the ladder creak as Connor jumped on, too, but she didn't look back. She knew she'd never get to the top if she cast so much as a glance all the way back down where she'd started from. Well, if she lost her grip and tumbled off, at least Connor would break her fall. Again.

Finally, when she thought sure her arms were going to break, when her ankle felt as if it had swollen up to the size of a basketball, she finally hit the top, hoisting herself through the opening. She crawled out onto a tiny platform, with a wrought-iron railing around it. She peered into the darkness of the passage. But all she saw was space.

And then something touched her.

"Aaaaaaee!" she screamed, but it was only Connor, barely breaking a sweat as he cleared the ladder.

"We're at the top of a circular staircase. It leads back down to the passage we were in before," he said flatly, leaning over her to look down. "I saw it when I was there by myself, before your rather dramatic entrance."

"A ladder up and then a circular staircase back down?" she said doubtfully. Her ankle was throbbing, and she doubted it could handle any weight now at all, not even just a touch. How was she going to negotiate a perilous circular staircase? "What was the Commodore trying to do, set up an obstacle course?"

"Apparently." With a grim look of determination, Connor reached over and swung her up into his arms.

Well, that was a surprise. "What do you think you're doing?"

"Limping and jerking around like that, you're a lost cause. You'll fall and break a leg for sure." Carefully, he braced her weight against his body as he set his foot on the first step. "And if you're bound and determined to get out of here, and this is the only way, then I'm going to have to carry you, aren't I?"

"If I can't walk down by myself, how can you carry me?" she asked uneasily. "I don't think I like how the physics work out on this one."

But Connor didn't answer, just kept descending one step at a time. She squeezed her eyes shut, afraid to look, afraid of what she might see. She felt the edge of the stairs brush her foot or her arm more than once, and she was scared to death that they were both going to tumble headlong into the passage below.

She didn't know if he breathed a sigh of relief when his feet finally hit the flat surface of the tunnel floor, but she certainly did. Oddly enough, he didn't put her down, just started marching into the passage with her still aboard as cargo.

"What's this? You can't carry me the whole way!"

"If it's the only way to keep you out of trouble, I may have to," he muttered.

"But there's something I need," she protested, wiggling enough to try and turn him around. "There was a book that should've come flying out of my Aunt Petunia's closet when I did. Did you see it?"

"I felt it. Right on my head."

"Go back for it," she ordered. "It's important."

"Okay, okay." Shaking his head, he backtracked far enough to set her down on the bottom step, not bothering to be particularly gentle about it. And then he poked around in the darkness, until he finally came up with the book. *"The Good Witch's Guide to Life?"* he inquired, squinting down at the spine. "What do you need that for?"

"I just do," she said flatly. "Can you give it to me, please?"

He handed over the sturdy volume, and she half raised herself, ready to be lifted back into his embrace. But he paused, asking dryly, "Do you want any of the shoes, too, while we're at it? I'd hate to have to come back later."

"No, I don't need any of the shoes."

Meekly cradling her precious book, she hopped back into the security of his arms. It really was awfully nice of him to haul her around like this, and it almost made her forget the humiliating fact that her body burned for him, both in the real world and in that murky, haunting kingdom of dreams. And he knew it.

She could almost forget it, but not quite. Bumping along in his arms, with one hand curled around his neck, with his heart beating so close to her own, remembering was a lot easier than forgetting.

Finally, after they'd spiraled downward in the secret passage so close and so long that she thought she might explode, past a mysterious little door that Connor claimed didn't open, past another rickety set of stairs and around a big curve, finally they reached the back of the bookcase, which, thank God, was still standing open a crack.

Connor angled them both through the opening, and Saskia saw the welcome sight of her own library. She felt like jumping down and kissing the Persian carpet. But she couldn't resist a glance back over his shoulder, just to sneak a peak at the bookcase standing open like that.

"It's amazing, isn't it?" she mused. "I mean, there's a whole other world behind my bookcase."

As Connor was about to answer, however, a fat volume from somewhere high above them came lurching off its shelf, landing not two feet from Saskia.

"How did that happen?" she asked, shielding her head as she looked up to see where the mysterious jumping book had come from.

As they watched, incredulous, another book came sailing down, and then another. It was like watching a series of contestants line up for the high dive, and then, one after the other, take the plunge.

As books cascaded around them, piling up around their feet, Connor swore under his breath. "What else?" he muttered. "What else can happen?"

Still holding Saskia secure, he ducked his head and made a beeline out of the turbulent world of the library. But as the heavy doors swung closed behind them, all they heard was the deafening echo of a completely silent room.

HE KNOCKED POLITELY on her bedroom door.

"Go away," she said immediately.

"It's me," he called. "Connor."

"I know it's you. Who else would it be?"

The Ghost of Christmas Past? In this house, anything was possible.

"Go away," she said. "I'm busy."

"How busy can you be, if you're lying in bed with a sprained ankle?"

"Busy enough that I don't want you barging into my bedroom."

"Look, Saskia—"

"Go away!" she said more forcefully.

"But we need to talk." He was getting desperate. "About why you and I are having the same dream. About Isabelle. About how we could both stumble over secret doors at the exact same moment. About the mysterious flying books in the library. There has to be some explanation for all of this, and we're the only ones who can sort it out."

"But if you would just leave me alone for five minutes, we might not have to," she wailed.

It was frustrating to talk to a door when there was a much more appealing woman on the other side of it. "What sense does that make?"

"Trust me."

"How can I trust you if I don't know what you're doing?"

"Look, Connor," she shouted, "you're the one who hauled me up here and insisted I go to bed. You're the one who told me I needed to lie down and rest my foot. Now leave me alone so I can do it."

He stood outside that blasted door for a long moment, contemplating splintering it with his bare hands. All he could hear from inside was the shuffling of pages, and maybe a pen scratching against paper. Since when had reading and writing become so important that she couldn't talk to him first, when their very lives might be at stake?

"Go away, Connor," she said again.

He considered it.

"Can't you find anything to do to occupy yourself?" she asked. "We can talk tomorrow, after... Well, after I put together what I need to."

"I suppose that will have to do." He paused. "And tomorrow we'll discuss all the strange things that have been happening, right? Tomorrow we will thrash this out."

"I hope we won't have to," she mumbled, but he heard every word.

As he started to leave, giving in to the inevitable, she called after him, "Oh, and Connor? If you're going to eat anything in this house, make sure Aunt Primrose is the one doing the cooking. Not Petunia. That's very important, okay?"

"Why? Does Petunia have a penchant for arsenic or something?"

"Don't argue, and don't make fun of me," she said with a testy edge. "Just don't eat anything prepared by Petunia, do you hear me?"

"Maybe I should leave the house and find a McDonald's," he said grimly.

"That's a good idea."

"Maybe I should leave the house and check into a hotel."

"That's a great idea!"

As if he would leave her here at the mercy of... well, at the mercy of whatever the hell was happening in this house.

"I'm staying," he said flatly. "And I don't believe in ghosts."

"Who said anything about ghosts?"

Connor stuck his hands in his pockets, setting his jaw pensively as he shuffled down the hall. Every time he thought things had become as bizarre as they possibly could, Saskia came up with a new wrinkle of weirdness.

"WHAT ARE YOU DOING?" Saskia demanded. She rushed over and snatched the bowl right out of Aunt Petunia's hand. "I was only gone for five minutes."

"I was trying to help," Petunia responded, with such a hurt look on her face that Saskia felt like a real criminal for yelling at her. Especially when she glanced down and saw only plain green beans in the dish, just the way she'd left them.

"I told you, tonight *I* am doing dinner all by myself," Saskia reminded her aunt. "When I left, I asked you not to touch anything, remember? I was only gone long enough to run upstairs and change my clothes."

"And you look lovely, too. I know Mr. Wynn is going to be so pleased."

"You really think so?" She was wearing a black cotton dress with a portrait collar and big buttons down the front, and she felt sort of conspicuous. But for some reason, she'd felt that it was important to be dressed up tonight. "Everything has to be perfect," she said under her breath.

She glanced at the open book on the counter, running through the ingredients again to make sure she hadn't forgotten anything.

But Petunia paid no attention. Giggling, she tossed her soft violet curls gaily. "He's smitten, that's for sure. Why, he's been so anxious to see you, my dear, all day long he's acted like a caged bear at the zoo. And last night, too. Why, do you know he actually played canasta with me and your Aunt Primrose, just to take his mind off you? We won quite a bit of money from him, too," she confided.

"That's nice."

"I think your strategy of being rather mysterious and elusive was simply brilliant. Such a good idea. Originally I thought it would be better if you spent some time together, but I see now that you were right. Absence makes the heart grow fonder, after all."

"Uh-huh," she said vacantly. "Dill weed, ginseng, calendula, rue, all together, steeped in a stew. Okay, I've got all that." Although what this awful stew was going to taste like, she had no idea. "Take two bites, and he'll love you true. But if you eat three, your heart will be free." She took a deep breath. "I certainly hope so. Although it doesn't say how you get them to eat exactly three bites. I wonder if that means any three bites, or only big ones. I mean, a tiny piece of carrot would hardly count, would it?"

"What did you say, dear?" Petunia asked, leaning over the kettle to smell the fumes rising off the stew.

"Don't do that, Aunt Petunia!" she cried, grabbing the whole pot out of the way. "You don't know what might happen."

Her aunt cocked her curls to one side. "You are very strange tonight, Saskia. And what is that book you keep fussing over? It doesn't look like your regular cookbook, dear."

"That's because it's a new one." She pushed the book behind her, well out of sight. "I thought Connor would like more, meaty things that we usually eat."

"And isn't that thoughtful of you?"

"Isn't it?" Saskia smiled weakly. "Why don't you go and fetch him, Aunt Petunia? I think everything is almost ready."

"Don't forget the beans," Petunia said mysteriously, but she disappeared from the kitchen on cue, leaving Saskia alone with her pots and pans.

She took another deep breath, inventorying everything in her mind rapidly, trying to think if there was anything she could possibly have missed. The stew was supposed to counteract the first love spell, while the fragrant frangipani candles on the dining-room table were intended to stop the erotic dreams in their tracks. They were actually designed for succubi and nightmares, but that was close enough.

Meanwhile, she was also brewing tea like mad, just in case there was anything to Madame Renata's theory about ghosts on the loose.

"This is never going to work." She leaned her hip against the counter, trying not to panic. But there were too many odd things happening to even be sure what she was dealing with.

Her first simple idea to reverse her aunts' spell had gone up in smoke, vanquished as soon as she read the book and realized that messing with dreams was different from stopping magic-induced lust, and that making books return to their shelves was way out of her league.

"Almonds," she said suddenly. The green beans were supposed to have almonds, which *The Good Witch's Guide* said would act as protection against other people's spells of all varieties. If she could just get enough almonds down Connor, maybe he'd be safe from further meddling by her aunts.

In a rush, she tossed in the slivered almonds, and fixed up the beans. Then, with everything ready to go, she arranged it all in the serving dishes. With fragrant, possibly deadly food in hand, she swung through the door to the dining room.

Primrose and Madame Renata were in their places, eagerly awaiting the meal, smiling through the haze from the frangipani candles burning away in the middle of the table. Saskia bit back a cough. Yuck. That wasn't the right scent for dinner at all.

Worse yet, there was no Petunia. And no Connor.

"Where are they?" she asked anxiously, trying to balance her silver chafing dish of green beans as she shoved aside a basket of rolls near her own place at the foot of the table.

Funny, she didn't remember sticking fennel seed on her bread before she baked it. And the seeds appeared to only be on the top roll. Where had all that fennel come from?

"Here, let me," Primrose interrupted, juggling a different dish and making a spot for the tureen of stew. "Where's the ladle, dear?"

"Oh, in the drawer in the sideboard, with the silver."

But halfway to the ladle, a shiver went up the back of her spine. She turned.

Connor had arrived.

Tall, impossibly good-looking, wearing a jacket and tie, he filled the whole dining room doorway. Forget the dinner. He looked good enough to eat.

"Uh, sit down," she said breathlessly, wondering if her knees were knocking, or if that was just her heart, rattling against her ribs.

He arched an eyebrow, lazily moseying over to a chair next to hers. "How's your ankle?"

"Much better, thank you." She gazed at him shyly. "I, uh, found a sort of poultice that worked wonders. It feels fine now."

"Well, in that dress, no one's going to be looking at your ankle."

Was that good? "Oh," she murmured.

His eyes swept the table, with its assorted dishes. "By the way, am I allowed to eat tonight?"

"What?"

"Eat. Here. Aren't I supposed to ask who's cooking before I eat?"

"Oh, right." She smiled. But her hand shook as she poured his wine, and a few deep red drops splattered on the white tablecloth. "I'm cooking tonight. That's the whole point."

"Then why do I feel so unsafe?"

Because we're in the same room again, and every time that happens, things go wrong. "Tonight, nothing is going to go wrong," she said severely. "Everything is going to work."

He flashed her a very strange look, and she repeated to herself, reciting in an inarticulate undertone, *Take two bites, and he'll love you true. But if you eat three, your heart will be free.*

Did she want his heart to be free? *Free to make his own choices,* she told herself. Free to dream in peace, without her or Isabelle sneaking in there.

Resolute, she passed him the pot of stew. "Eat up."

But just as he took the tureen out of her hand, just as his fingers brushed hers, a crash of thunder filled the room. Saskia flinched. Rain lashed against the windows, and the chandelier above the table began to sway back and forth eerily.

"Where did that come from?" she asked shakily. "It's been nice all day."

There was no answer, just another boom of thunder, a slash of lightning. And then the bulbs in the chandelier faded and died completely, leaving the dining room with only the vague flicker of the frangipani candles to light it.

"Well, at least it happened after all the food was cooked," Petunia chirped into the darkness.

Saskia could hear Primrose scurrying along the edge of the table, feeling her way to the sideboard. She came back with two ornate silver candelabra that she set up on the long, heavy table to augment the other candles.

As the wind and rain pounded outside, as the soft light from the candles waved and blinked, the atmosphere in the dining room became even more Gothic, even more strained.

Of course, Madame Renata's appetite was as prodigious as ever, and she chowed down with gusto, ignoring the weather and the spooky ambience.

Across from the medium, Primrose glanced around at her dinner companions with her usual expression of fear and apprehension, while Petunia chattered away, as if it were all a great adventure.

And Connor just sat there, moodily staring at Saskia. He looked as if he were trying to read her mind, but not having much success.

As the storm howled and moaned, Banquo the cat appeared from out of nowhere, taking up a post in the window, flapping the lace curtain with his tail. Saskia hadn't quite recovered her equanimity yet, and Banquo's appearance did nothing to settle her nerves.

But she knew that the sooner they got this over with, the sooner her pulse would stop racing, the sooner she'd stop imagining dire things every time a spot of bad weather kicked up.

"Why don't we eat before everything gets cold?" she offered, even though Madame Renata was already on to her third helping. "Here, Connor, try this." Carefully, she ladled three spoonfuls of stew onto his plate.

"I'm perfectly capable of serving myself, you know."

She glared at him, dumping a big pile of green beans, heavy on the almonds, all over his plate. "Be quiet. Eat your food. All of it. Just do it, will you?"

"You're certainly bossy tonight," he muttered. He peered down at his plate, as if trying to make out shapes in the shadows, but he didn't venture a bite.

"Eat it," she hissed. "Every bite."

"Saskia!" On her left, Primrose sounded scandalized. "What's gotten into you? Where are your manners?"

Meanwhile, Petunia leapt up from her place and sprinted all the way around the table to offer Connor a piece of bread. Bypassing Renata and Primrose, she stood over Connor, watching him like a hawk, smiling a big smile, as he reluctantly took the top roll in the basket, the one that was peeking out from between the folds of a napkin. The one with all the seeds.

Those seeds, put together with Petunia's peculiar race to give Connor a roll, was enough to make Saskia very suspicious.

"Did you make the bread, Aunt Petunia?" she asked warily.

"No, dear, you did." Petunia smiled sweetly. "Don't you remember?"

"I remember making it, but I didn't put any seeds on it. Fennel, is it?"

"Something like that. I thought it would add a little zest." Slyly, she added, "But just on Connor's. I made a special roll, just for him."

"How could you?" Saskia snapped, sending her aunt a lethal glare.

She was dying to ask what was on there and what it was for, but not in front of Connor. He gazed dubiously at the bread in his hand, finally setting it aside, but there was no way she was going to chance him forgetting and eating it later. She refused to allow Petunia's concoctions to screw up her own carefully hatched plans.

Snatching up the ladle from the stew, Saskia leaned way over him, pretending that she was reaching for the tureen. But at the last moment, she batted his roll completely off the table, smacking it with her ladle. It went sailing away into the shadows, and only the cat moved to find it.

"Sorry," she said sweetly. "Let me get you another one." And then she grabbed Petunia's unused, un-seeded bread right off her plate and stuck it on Connor's.

As Connor gave Saskia a suspicious glance, Petunia made a funny "humph" noise and stalked back to the kitchen. Didn't she realize how obvious her little game was?

Apparently not. As the meal progressed, Aunt Petunia kept trooping back and forth with different "treats" which she tried to fob off on Connor. But Saskia was every bit as determined as her demented aunt.

Before Connor took a bite of anything Petunia offered, Saskia somehow managed to steal it, move it, knock it over or exchange it.

"Why aren't you eating your stew?" she asked with a big smile. "Or your green beans? They're good for you."

But he just narrowed his eyes at her.

"Here, Connor," Petunia said sympathetically. "You don't want that. It's all cold." She seized the plate right out from under his nose. "Let me make you something else."

"Give that back," Saskia demanded, blocking her aunt's exit.

"No," Petunia returned stubbornly. "It's cold. It's unappealing. I'll just whip him up a nice plate of roast beef and mashed potatoes. It won't take a minute."

"He wants this plate," Saskia insisted. "Let's give Connor what he wants, shall we?"

"I think he wants roast beef!"

Petunia tried to weave around her niece, plate in hand, but Saskia was too quick for her. As they both grabbed for it, the plate stuck there in midair, stew and green beans sliding ominously near the edge, with both of them pulling and pushing at it.

"How nice that you're both so concerned with my food," Connor said acidly.

"We just want you to have the best," Saskia said quickly.

"Exactly," her aunt chorused.

"And that's why Aunt Petunia is going to give you back your plate. Isn't she?"

"I most certainly am not."

"Then I will take this one back to the kitchen, and bring Connor a fresh one."

"I will," Petunia volunteered.

"Oh, no, you won't."

"Yes, yes, I will. I don't mind."

"Forget it," he said abruptly, pushing back his chair and rising from the table. "What do you think I am, nuts?"

Saskia paused in mid-shove. Politely, she asked, "Whatever do you mean?"

His eyebrows drew together darkly. "I'd have to have an IQ hovering around four not to notice what you two are doing. I wouldn't eat your food if the surgeon general herself gave it her personal seal of approval."

"Well, there's no need to be surly," Aunt Petunia put in.

"I'm not being surly," he growled. "I'm hungry, and I'm absolutely fed up."

"How is that possible?" Primrose inquired, blinking at him.

With a grim look of determination, Connor caught Saskia in one hand and a candelabra off the table with the other. He then proceeded to drag her along behind him, past the long table and out of the dining room. "Come on, Saskia. We're getting out of here."

"We are? Where are we going?"

He didn't answer, but he did pause to stow the candlestick on a handy table as they neared the front hallway. Without bothering with preliminaries, he asked tersely, "Do you have a car?"

"Of course."

"Give me your keys." He held out his hand. "Your keys?"

She'd never seen him like this. Slowly, she pulled her car keys off a hook in the entryway and handed them over. "Where are we going?"

"Away from here," he said with feeling. Swinging open the heavy front door, tackling the rain and wind head-on, Connor grabbed her hand and hauled her along behind him again. "We're going somewhere where we can get a decent meal, and then we're going to see if we can't come up with a few hard truths."

"Like what?"

"Like what the hell is going on around here, and why you people are trying to poison me."

Chapter Nine

"You know I wasn't trying to poison you."

Connor flashed her a sardonic look as he dug back into his steak. "Then what were you doing?"

"I-I don't know how to explain."

"Try me."

"Well..."

It was certainly a lot easier to be civil in the genteel, polished surroundings of the grand dining room at the Jekyll Island Club, where the only distractions were the quiet hum of other people's conversations, and the discreet clinking of cutlery and wineglasses. But it was even harder to tell him that her aunts thought they were witches, and that she was also convinced now.

Here, away from the house, life was simply too comfortable, too reasonable for any of that to make sense. Saskia felt herself unwinding, enjoying the place and Connor. The drive over had been a bit tense, but now he, too, seemed much less anxious, much more kindly disposed to her, than he had back at Wynn-wood.

It was no wonder. The Jekyll Island Club, once again a fashionable resort hotel, was restored to all of the grace it had held back in the days when influential millionaires had built their private haven.

When she'd made her first trip to the island to visit Aunt Poppy, she'd been enchanted by the charming conical tower on the wharf side of the hotel; the wide white porch with its trailing flowers and wicker rockers; the tall palm trees and live oaks that gave the grounds their Southern atmosphere. The whole place bespoke class and tranquility, nothing overdone, just right.

And when she'd come up with her bed-and-breakfast plan, she'd hoped to blend in in some small way with the sterling ambience of the Jekyll Island Club. Those who wanted relaxation and elegance could stay at the club. But she hoped that a few more adventurous souls might wander out to Wynnwood, all by itself on the tip of the island, with its more eccentric charms.

Talk about eccentric. After this trip, she was sure Connor would be willing to verify its eccentricities firsthand.

"Come on," he prompted, "spill it. What were you and Petunia trying to do at dinner tonight? If not poison me, I mean."

"Well," she said delicately, trying to decide how best to phrase this. "You might say we were at cross-purposes."

"That much I guessed. Go on."

"All right. I guess I'm just going to have to come right out with it." She took a deep breath. "The first night you got there, my aunts cast a spell in the attic.''

There was a long moment of silence. "A what?" he said finally.

"A spell.'' She chewed her lip. "As it happens, it was a love spell. Petunia made up a poem and Primrose danced around with a tambourine.''

"Okay.'' He seemed to be having difficulty picturing that, and she couldn't blame him. "And then what?''

"And then what?'' Saskia looked around hastily, dropping her voice before she whispered, "And then it worked!''

"Oh, come on.''

"No, I'm serious.'' She leaned over closer. "Think about it. It was right after they cast their spell that you got all weird and tried to pull me into bed with you, and then only a little later that the two of us had that fantastic dream.''

"Yeah,'' he said roughly, "I remember.''

Saskia shivered. "So do I. Anyway, then we fell into the secret passage at exactly the same time, and you know what happened then.''

We fell onto the ground like a couple of panting, love-crazed animals. In about three seconds flat, your skirt was gone, my shirt was gone and we were all over each other.

She knew her face had turned six shades of red just thinking about it.

His gaze held a touch of hunger. "Yes, I know exactly what happened then.''

"I mean, is that like you? It's not like me.''

"Okay, so it's not like me, either." He clenched his jaw. "But that doesn't mean that magic spells are possible. What is this? Sleeping Beauty?"

"Look, I didn't want to believe it, either, but—"

"And from your aunts? Saskia," he said in a low, persuasive tone, and he pulled her hands into his. "Saskia, it just isn't possible. Even if there were such things as magic spells, those two couldn't do them. They couldn't bewitch their way out of a paper bag."

"That's what I thought at first. But then..." She shook her head. "Well, who knows? Madame Renata thinks it's a ghost. I heard her say that she thought they let the Commodore loose the night of the séance. I suppose that would explain the flying books, and maybe even your half of the dream. But not mine." Here eyes were imploring. "And how do you explain the feeling I got the first time we met that I already knew you?"

"I felt the same way." He narrowed his eyes. "But that happened *before* the love potion."

"You're right!" She put a hand over her open mouth. "Oh, no. Then that means..."

"This is too weird," he murmured.

"Oh, Connor, I'm so sorry." Her words spilling out faster now, Saskia edged closer. "Why didn't I realize? The spooky stuff started happening *before* they cast their spell. I really thought that stupid incantation in the attic did all of it, and that's why I tried to reverse it."

"Reverse it?"

She hesitated again. "You remember *The Good Witch's Guide?* Well, I found a recipe for taking away love spells. And I'm a very good cook, so I thought I could—"

"Run up to the attic and start pounding on your own tambourine?" he asked doubtfully.

"No, of course not. You had to eat it." She added, "So I mixed it into your stew."

"You put something in my stew to make me *not* fall in love with you?" He rubbed his palm over his forehead, as if he were having trouble focusing. "You really thought that sticking some fungus or something in my food would make me hate you? Well, I guess there's a certain logic to that, if," he added plainly, "I'd known what you were doing at the time."

"I wasn't trying to make you hate me. I wasn't even trying to make you not fall in love with me." This was so complicated; she felt as if she were picking her way through a mine field. "I was only trying to make you not fall in love with me *because of some crazy spell of my aunts*. It wouldn't be right. Not like that. I mean, I would've felt like a fake. A horrible fraud. Not that I'm suggesting I did want you to fall in love with me," she said in a rush.

"Of course not."

"But if I did, well, I wouldn't want it that way. So I had to try to reverse their spell with one of my own. Does that make sense?"

"Kind of. In a very warped way." He let out a long breath. "Just don't do it again, okay? I can dodge Aunt Petunia, but the two of you together is a pretty tough act."

She couldn't believe he was taking it this well. "But I thought you'd be really angry. About their spell *and* mine."

"What would it serve me to be angry? It's not like that kind of thing has even the remotest chance of working. But next time, don't try to solve things for me. Share it. You know—two heads are better than one." A cynical smile played around the corners of his mouth. "At least it would've saved all those games with my food. You know, you swatted my roll clear across the room."

"Sorry."

"What were those seeds, anyway?"

She lifted her shoulders in a shrug. "I don't know. Some kind of aphrodisiac is my best guess. Maybe Aunt Petunia didn't think the first spell was working fast enough, so she tried to hurry things up by socking you with a booster shot."

"An aphrodisiac?" he echoed. "Well, Aunt Petunia knows how to go right for the jugular, doesn't she?"

She couldn't keep the glimmer of amusement from her voice when she said, "I don't think it was your jugular she was interested in."

"Uh-huh."

"Connor," she began, trying hard to find some way to apologize, "I know this must all seem like some kind of circus to you. I mean, you come from such a respectable, conventional family. I'm sure no one tries witchcraft in the attic, and no one puts magic potions in your food. I hope you won't judge us too harshly."

"I'm not an ogre," he said softly. "Your family may not be like mine, but I have fair warning now. Whatever is happening, just tell me, okay?"

"I didn't think you'd believe me."

"I probably wouldn't have." And then he just stared at her for a long moment.

"What are you thinking?"

"That you're a lot more conventional than you want people to believe."

"Conventional? Me?" Where did that figure into a discussion of her trying to dose him with magic herbs?

"Yeah." A spark of mischief lit his crystal blue eyes. "You pretend to be one of the crazy Trueloves, no rules, no restrictions, but then you decide you don't want a man if your aunts got him for you with smoke and mirrors. 'It wouldn't be right,' you say, sounding just like Pollyanna. In fact, it sounds exactly like the kind of thing an honorable, totally respectable woman would say."

"And, you know," she said thoughtfully, "you're a lot *less* conventional than you want people to believe."

He blinked. "Me? Why?"

"Because you're sitting here chatting with me about witches and spells and ghosts, as if you might actually allow for the possibility. Why, we've gone right past the shared-dream thing—hypnosis, wasn't that your theory?—and vaulted into the spirit world. These sound like very improper thoughts for a practical, no-nonsense member of the Wynn family." She clicked her tongue. "Tsk, tsk. What would your mother say?"

"That you and I aren't so different after all."

He smiled, and she smiled back, and they shared a warm, surprisingly sweet moment.

He had the most amazing blue eyes, she thought, and a spectacular smile when he chose to use it. Why couldn't he have walked into her life under different circumstances, when the two of them could've gotten to know each other slowly, without so much insanity hanging over their heads?

"I like this place," he said, drawing out his words as he glanced around at the dining room. "Although I think our waiter thinks we're crazy. We've been here for hours, and we're not moving. But he doesn't know what we have to go back to."

"Why do you suppose he did it?" she asked idly, twirling her wine in its glass.

"Who? Did what?"

"The Commodore. Stuck his house out there all by itself. All the other millionaires either lived here at the club, or built their mansions in a nice, neat row right next door. But the Commodore chose to strike out on his own." Her gaze swept the room, dancing over the dark wood and the white tablecloths. "It seems strange he wouldn't want to live here, too."

"Maybe he wanted to hear the waves crashing on his very own shore."

"That's rather poetic for you, isn't it?" She eyed him more closely. "Now what do you really think?"

"Privacy, I guess." He shrugged. "Or maybe because of Isabelle."

Saskia sighed. She had been hoping to postpone talking about certain subjects for as long as possible.

But now that the subject of love potions had been disposed of without discord, she supposed everything else was fair game. She took a deep breath and forged ahead. "So you think she was a real person?"

"She's in the portrait, isn't she?"

"I know, but..." She didn't want to say it. "But she looks just like *me!*"

Connor cocked an eyebrow. "And that makes her somehow unreal?"

"I don't know." Saskia took a long sip of wine. It was going to her head, making her feel flushed, warm, a little woozy.

"What did you think, your aunts painted up a picture and stuck it in the secret room, just to fool you?"

"I wouldn't put it past them," she muttered.

"And I look like the Commodore," he went on. "What about that?"

"Well, you're supposed to. You're related, for goodness' sake."

He propped his chin in his hand and just gazed at her, with enough heat to curl her hair. "Maybe you're related to Isabelle."

"Oh, right. You think just because my family is unorthodox, we don't keep track of our gene pool." Head high, she informed him coolly, "There are not that many branches on my family tree. Because of the curse, I suppose."

"A curse, did you say?"

She ignored the question. "I know who my ancestors were, and none of them was Isabelle. She couldn't be from the Brueghel side, because my father came over straight from Holland, and then went back after he left my mother. As far as I know, that is. I was, what, three months old?''

"I'm sorry," he said penitently, and he really did sound sorry.

"Well, if you must know, that's part of the curse." As long as they were putting everything on the table, Saskia decided to just come out with it. A few hard truths, wasn't that what he'd said? "It's all silliness, anyway, but my aunts believe there is a curse on True-love women, and they don't stay married long as a result. My mother was no exception. Same for Aunt Poppy and your cousin Bunky, who didn't last past the honeymoon. I don't know who it's harder on—the women who are left behind, or the men the curse kills off.''

"How very strange."

"Yes, it really is." She leaned closer, warming up to her subject. "And neither Petunia nor Primrose ever married. My grandmother was fine, though, but then she wasn't a Truelove—she just married one. Octavia Des Moulins, the famous actress.''

He obviously had no clue what she was talking about.

"My grandparents on the Truelove side," she told him. "Octavia Des Moulins and Junius Brutus True-love. They were famous Shakespearean actors of their time. In fact, the whole family was full of actors and magicians, on both sides, always traveling around, doing tours of exotic places. And he had a sister, but don't worry—she wasn't named Isabelle. It was Ophelia or Desdemona or something dramatic like that.''

His expression was faintly appalled. "You really do have a bizarre family."

"Just because my great-aunt was named Desdemona?"

"Of course not. I was speaking about the traveling troupes of actors and magicians. No wonder your aunts think they're witches."

"Well, they were raised to be eccentric. It's part of being a Truelove," she said proudly. "Did you expect us to act like everybody else?"

Connor's eyes narrowed as he watched her steadily across the table. "It's amazing how much you look like Isabelle when you lift your chin and act all superior and smug that way."

She regarded him for a moment. "Don't you mean she looks like me?"

For a stodgy, stuffy businessman who had not grown up with Trueloves, he was fairly quick on the uptake. "Absolutely."

"Since I've demonstrated that the resemblance is not familial, I suppose that means it's just a coincidence. But a pretty strange one, don't you think?"

"Saskia, what hasn't been strange since the day we met?"

"Well, there is that." She signaled the waiter for another glass of wine. "So if we assume that Isabelle was a real person, then who was she?"

"All I know about are the Isabelle bronzes."

Her ears perked up. Even the sound of the word was intriguing. *Bronzes*. "What are they?"

"I don't know." Connor chewed his lip thoughtfully. "But that was originally why I came down here, to find out about the Isabelle bronzes."

Wryly, she noted, "I thought you came to kick me and my aunts out of Wynnwood for making a nuisance of ourselves."

"I was never going to kick you out," he maintained. "I just wanted to make you stop all the hocus-pocus stuff. But now that I've stayed there, I know that's impossible. Even if you didn't create mischief, somebody—or something—would."

"Well, I'm glad you see that." She managed a small smile. "So what's this about bronzes? And what do they have to do with Isabelle?"

"I assume she's the subject, but I really don't know. All I found was a receipt for an ungodly amount of money, paid to Gabriel Roques. Have you ever heard of him?"

She shook her head.

"He was a famous artist, one of those guys who lived in turn-of-the-century Paris, like Toulouse-Lautrec and some others. They made their names painting posters for the nightclubs, and they called themselves bohemians, referring to their life-style, not ethnic origin."

"I know that," she returned smartly.

"He's actually quite famous, more for his portraits and sculptures of New York society women than his original posters, but still very well-known. Not as famous as Octavia Des Jardins and Junius Plautus Truelove, of course—"

"It's Octavia Des *Moulins* and Junius *Brutus* True-love," she interrupted.

A grin flashed over his lips for a fraction of a second, and she got the definite idea that he was teasing her. But then he continued with his fine-art lecture. "So my guess is that the Commodore paid Gabriel Roques to sculpt a whole series of bronze statues of Isabelle, and he did it while she was staying at Wynn-wood. They'd be worth quite a bit of money." He raised an eyebrow. "Quite a bit."

"And is that why you were looking for them?"

"The money? No," he said shortly. "I told myself that at the beginning, but it wasn't true. No, from the moment her name jumped off the page at me, I knew I had to look for those statues." He mused, "I don't really know why."

"The same reason we both dreamed about her on the same night, I suppose." Saskia shivered. "Destiny. Karma. Forces beyond our control."

"I've been wondering about the same thing," he said, proceeding cautiously, watching her intently. "If our dreams really were identical, and we both think that they were, then we know one thing about Isabelle, don't we?"

"What's that?"

"That she was the Commodore's lover." His voice seemed to have developed a catch. "I don't know what you saw, but from what I dreamed, there doesn't seem to be any doubt of that."

Details of that fabulous dream began to waft back into her brain. Slowly, concentrating hard to remember only the facts and none of the torchy parts, she said, "He asked her to marry him. I remember that."

"But she didn't."

"Well, not then, anyway. But maybe later she said yes," she offered hopefully.

He shook his head. "Nope. He never married her."

Saskia leaned forward, ready to do battle. It should mean nothing to her if the Commodore and Isabelle hadn't lived happily ever after, but suddenly the resolution of their story seemed very important. "You can't know that for sure," she argued. "All we saw was one short scene from their lives. Maybe later they patched up their differences and tied the knot."

"He was my great-grandfather, remember? Don't you think I know who he was married to?" Connor asked in a chilly tone. "My great-grandmother was a very rich, very dull, very proper woman named Margaret Willingsworth. She was the daughter of an undersecretary of the navy, and if her pictures are any indication, she looked very much on the order of a battleship."

"But—" she tried.

Connor charged on. "They had two children, both boys. First was Willingsworth, called Willie, who was my grandfather. The other one was Edwin, called Neddy, whose major claim to fame was that he fathered the infamous Edward Buchanan Wynn, also known as Bunky. Margaret outlived her husband by about thirty years—too mean to die, my mother always says. And she was it as far as wives go for the Commodore."

"Well, maybe he had a marriage you don't know about." Saskia frowned at him. "Secret rooms, secret passageways—why not a secret marriage?"

"Don't be absurd," he shot back. "He was a Wynn. As a matter of fact, he was the stuffiest and most repressed of the bunch. He would never have married a woman like Isabelle in the first place—"

"A woman like Isabelle?" she interrupted. "You mean all that nonsense about smoking cigarettes and wearing pants in public? I mean, how silly can you get? If he couldn't look past a few innocent quirks to be with the woman he loved, then what kind of a wimp was he?"

"He wanted to get married," Connor said angrily. "She was the one who refused."

"Only because she knew that he would be miserable married to her because he was such a puffed-up prig!"

"Excuse me," their waiter said kindly. "But you seem to be shouting. Could you please keep your voices down so our other patrons can enjoy their dinner?"

Saskia felt her face flame. "Yes, of course."

Connor looked every bit as embarrassed as she was. "It seems we both remember the dream quite vividly," he commented. "Down to the argument they were having."

"But it seems so pointless for us to be fighting it over again on their behalf. I mean," she murmured, "they've been dead a long time."

"I guess it just means we both took the dream seriously."

"It hits home, doesn't it?" Saskia phrased her words carefully. "They weren't so different from you and me."

"What do you mean?"

Saskia sat back in her chair, feeling gloomy all of a sudden. "The whole thing about her not being the right sort of person and him being all wrapped up in his social standing. It's not all that far from the argument we had in the parlor, when you hadn't even been in the house ten minutes."

"Oh, come on."

"No, I mean it. Don't you remember all that nonsense about how I was desecrating your family name by running a haunted bed-and-breakfast? And how Poppy, being a lowly Truelove, wasn't good enough to marry a Wynn. It sounds exactly like something the Commodore would've said."

"Maybe that's why we're reliving it," he said softly. His eyes were a moodier blue when he caught her gaze again. "Have you thought of that?"

"No." She licked her lip. "It hadn't occurred to me. But, Connor, that would presuppose that you and I...that we..."

"Are going to be lovers, like they were?" He placed his longer, stronger hand over hers where it rested on the tablecloth, and he leaned in, taking her fingers, bringing them up to his lips. "But, Saskia," he whispered, and she could feel the hot puffs of his breath on the back of her hand, "we already are."

She could barely manage to get out a gruff whisper; her voice seemed to have abandoned her. "In the dream, you mean? But that wasn't real."

"It felt real to me." His lips barely grazed her skin, and she closed her eyes, trying to swallow, trying to breathe.

She felt as if she were lit up from the inside out. He'd barely touched her, and yet she was so caught up in whatever erotic lasers were beaming back and forth that she could hardly move.

Saskia licked her lip. She wanted him. This was neither the time nor the place for that decision, and there were about a hundred obstacles looming large in her path. This was the looniest, least sensible thing she'd ever contemplated in her whole, illogical life.

But she wanted Connor Wynn.

And she decided right then and there that she was going to have him, whether or not it involved the assistance of every love potion in the western hemisphere.

He brushed his mouth back and forth over her fingers, and her whole arm buzzed with familiar electricity. Every time he touched her, it was there again.

"Connor," she ventured. "About those dreams. Did you have one last night?"

"No, I didn't." As he looked up from her hand, his narrow lips curved into a naughty smile. "Slept like a baby. It was very disappointing."

"I didn't have one, either. I can't figure out why, though." She pursed her lips. "I thought it would be a relief not to. But it was almost worse this way."

"Did you dislike it that much?"

She hesitated, but in the end she had to be honest. "No. I didn't. That was what frightened me. It was wonderful."

"Wonderful," he echoed.

"Tonight, I burned a special kind of candle to try to stop them from coming again. Do you suppose it will work?"

"Let's hope not." He stood, drawing her up into his arms as if he were pulling her into a dance. "Right now, Saskia, I would give anything I own to have another one of those dreams."

And then he kissed her.

It was sweet and gentle, a little too long for propriety's sake in the middle of a restaurant, but she didn't care. She kissed him back.

Until he broke away suddenly. He stumbled back a step, almost knocking into a nearby table, and his gaze seemed to jump around the room, searching here and there, as if he were confused.

"Connor? What is it?" she asked, but he didn't answer.

HE TURNED, AND EVERYTHING in the dining room shifted, like the inside of a kaleidoscope. Where there had been tables and dinner guests a moment ago, now women in fancy dresses swished and swayed. He saw a hazy blur of chandeliers, champagne glasses, fresh flowers, waiters in tailcoats, and he heard the faint, off-kilter strains of a string quartet, over in one corner.

"A dance," he whispered. "A dance at the club."

Across the room, J. P. Morgan chatted amiably with W. K. Vanderbilt and Joseph Pulitzer. Off to one side, portly President McKinley stood conferring with his host on the island, Frederick Baker.

But he cared nothing for presidents and puffed-up millionaires. Where was Isabelle?

He smiled with anticipation, hoping desperately that she would attend tonight's soirée. *I have the power and the influence,* he had assured her, *if you come as my guest, none will dare speak against you.*

And when she arrived, and they danced together for all the world to see, she could no longer make her silly objections to his proposal. Isabelle would have to admit that she did fit in, that her mere presence on his arm was not a scandal, and that they would have the happiest marriage in the whole social register.

He sensed she was there before he saw her. Hope and love filled his heart as he turned, eager to greet her.

She was beautiful, simply stunning, in a white lace dress and a long rope of pearls he had given her for her birthday. He smiled, charging across the ballroom, offering his arm.

But suddenly everything seemed to have darkened, changed. Isabelle flushed, and her smile disappeared.

As he hesitated there in the grand dining room of the Jekyll Island Club, he heard the faint whispers of a conversation behind him.

"...Isabelle Harris," a matron hissed. "Father lost all his money... So very pretty...so very shocking..."

"...tried to steal Marjorie Van Hamm's husband right out from under her. But Marjorie won in the end." Sniff. "That sort of girl never prospers..."

"Do you suppose she's got her hooks into poor Edmund Wynn now?"

His hands twisted into fists. But he stood there, powerless to stop the whispers.

The dancing couples faded back, receding into vague puffs of pale color in the periphery of his vision, as he stalked to where Isabelle still waited. He stood there, his eyes searching her face, but she wouldn't look at him.

That his Isabelle, his beautiful, spirited, vulnerable Isabelle, should be too wounded to meet his gaze... It was devastating. What had he done?

"My darling," he whispered, holding out his gloved hand. "Please dance with me. We will make it all right. You'll see."

"Oh, Edmund, how could you ask this of me?" And then, on the brink of tears, she whirled and left the ballroom.

He made a move to follow, as the faces around him seemed to melt into waxy horror, their mouths looping wide open into long O's. They were all staring, whispering, pointing.

This wasn't done. Men such as Commodore Edmund Wynn did not make public spectacles of their illicit lovers.

But then, everyone knew he was bit eccentric, with his house so far from the wharf. It was rumored that he'd built it way out there so he could smuggle his mistresses in and out without being seen.

"No!" he cried.

But he was confused, disoriented. Where was he now? What was happening? It was all so dark, so dim. He wrenched off his glove, lifting a hot hand to his forehead.

"Isabelle," he whispered, and the room went black.

COLD WATER SPLASHED across his face.

"Connor?"

"What happened?" he asked. He was sitting in an overstuffed chair in the lobby outside the restaurant, and he had no idea how he'd gotten there.

"I don't know." Saskia's expression was very concerned. "You kissed me, and then you kind of turned around a few times, like you were seeing something I wasn't. Finally, you charged over by the doorway, and then you sort of..." She let out a quick breath. "You just crumpled. Connor, you scared me to death. Are you all right? The maître d' got you into the chair, because I never would've been able to—"

"So you didn't see it? Any of it?"

"Any of what?"

"Isabelle and the dance. The Commodore wanted her there, but all these old biddies said terrible things, and she ran out crying. It was awful."

Her eyes were wide as they searched his face. "Another dream with the Commodore and Isabelle?"

He nodded.

"But... But I wasn't there. I didn't see any of it."

"It's worse than that, Saskia." Ignoring the stares from the hotel guests and diners milling around, he pulled her out onto the veranda, out into the cool air and the hard rain. "It happened away from Wynnwood." He gave her a tormented look. "If it can happen away from Wynnwood, that means it's following me around."

"It was just the dining room. It reminded you of..." But her voice trailed away.

"I've never been in that dining room. What could it possibly remind me of?" He ran a hand through his hair, pacing back and forth on the porch. "It was so real, Saskia, down to the sweat trickling into my collar points and President McKinley."

"President McKinley?"

"I don't even know what he looks like—me, Connor, doesn't, I mean—but I saw him in that ballroom. And I saw everything else, too, things I would have no way of knowing."

For those short moments, he had felt so much a part of that time period and way of life it was scary. Not to mention recognizing people he knew nothing about.

"But why?" he asked out loud. "Why am I seeing scenes from someone else's life, someone else's heartache?"

"I don't know."

"There's only one explanation." He didn't want to think it, but it was all he was left with.

"Well? What?"

"Maybe Madame Renata was right. Maybe they did let loose a restless spirit the night of the séance."

"But you can't mean—"

He nodded slowly. "I think I'm possessed by the ghost of the Commodore."

Chapter Ten

"Saskia, you're running around with a crazy man," he insisted. His long strides ate up the rainswept green lawns outside the ornate, old hotel buildings. "Everywhere I turn, I'm bombarded with memories that aren't my own. Over there," he said, flinging out an arm, "I see the Sans Souci apartments, and I think, 'Oh, I wonder if Cornelius Bliss is in.' Who the hell is Cornelius Bliss? Or there, that's the back of Indian Mound, one of the private cottages. Gordon McKay built it, but he sold it to William Rockefeller shortly before I left the island. Before *he* left the island," he corrected himself angrily.

"Connor, it doesn't matter," she tried, catching at his arm.

"Of course, it matters." He gave her a black look. "No poison herbs thrown in my stew are going to solve this."

"Stop it," she commanded. "Just stop it. You're right, it's scary. It's creepy. And now it's not just when we're asleep, and not just at Wynnwood. But there is one constant factor I've figured out."

"What's that?"

She held out a hand, letting the raindrops dance against her palm. "The weird stuff only happens when we're in the middle of a storm."

"Neither of us had nightmares last night. And there was no storm." He sighed deeply. "Maybe we could move to a desert."

Her hand to her mouth, she laughed out loud. "That's the spirit. Now you're thinking of solutions."

"Oh, Saskia." He swung around sharply, catching her and drawing her into his arms for a heartfelt hug. Into her hair, he murmured, "You shouldn't be here. I should let you go."

"Let me go? Do you think I would? What, are you crazy?"

"Don't ask," he muttered.

"I didn't mean it literally." She detached herself from his embrace but held on to his hand, giving it a quick squeeze. "I'm just so happy it's not the love potion. What a relief. Mere possession I can deal with."

But he only glowered at her.

"Listen to me, Connor. Whatever happens, whatever we need to do to sort this thing out, we're in this together."

"You don't have to—"

"Oh, yes, I do. When I twisted my ankle, you carried me the whole way down that horrible staircase, and the rest of the passage, too. That was teamwork." She took him by the lapels of his expensive suit and shook him. "So we'll share it. You know—two heads are better than one."

"That's not fair. You're using my own words against me."

"Who said I was fair?" With his lapels firmly in hand, Saskia tilted up and kissed him, hard.

It was a harsh, demanding kiss, with nothing soft or kind about it. She wanted him to know this had nothing to do with pity. He might be bewitched at the moment, but she didn't care.

Above her, his mouth was fierce and hot, as if he wanted to brand her more than kiss her. She was perfectly willing to be branded, and she wound her arms around his neck, angling closer, giving back as good as she got, matching his desire with more of her own.

And when it was done, when they had to break away, gasping for breath, she just looked at him.

"Well?" she asked.

"Well, I guess that was your way of telling me I don't have a choice. You're along for the ride."

"I knew that the first moment I saw you, all wet and cranky in my parlor. There was already this connection to you built into my heart." She began to laugh. "And now here you are, still wet and cranky. Not much changes, does it?"

"Everything has changed."

"Has it?" Saskia wasn't sure exactly what he was talking about, but she liked the sound of it on his lips. "Well, what next, partner?"

"First we get out of the rain," he said, casting a dark glance up at the sky, which was rumbling ominously, promising worse storms to come.

"Back to Wynnwood?"

But he was already charging across the grounds, headed under a live oak tree with low, sweeping bushes, back toward the gravel lot where they'd parked the car.

"If there's anywhere else you'd like to go, I'm game," he told her, as he swung open her door on the decrepit old station wagon. "Personally, I'd vote for running away somewhere and never coming back. What do you say? Tahiti? Paris? Alaska?"

She gulped. "Are you serious?"

"Perfectly," he said darkly.

"But I couldn't. My aunts—"

"Would muddle through. They'd love getting to be in charge of Wynnwood and all its supernatural treats."

"Probably. But I couldn't leave them." As he turned the key in the ignition, Saskia said softly, "You have to understand, they were all I had after my mother died. They practically raised me."

"So no trip to Tahiti?"

She shook her head. "No trip to Tahiti. But, Connor, I promise you we will cure you or cure the Commodore. Whatever it takes."

He gave her a quick kiss. "I do understand. You're being trustworthy and conventional again."

The island was small, and it only took a few minutes to negotiate the drive up the shore to Wynnwood. But then Connor left the motor running, gazing out through the rain at the dark house, letting the rhythmic slap of the windshield wipers break the silence, making no move to go inside.

"Well, here we are."

"Here we are."

"I don't want to go in there," he said. "Do you?"

"I'm scared out of my wits." She slumped down in her seat. "Will the books run out of the library and smack us? Will ghosts haunt us in our beds?"

"They already have."

"Oh, yeah."

"There is one solution."

"What's that?"

His voice dropped lower, softer. "Instead of tossing and turning in our lonely beds..."

She knew what was coming.

He sent her a sideways glance. "I'm sure we'd both feel a lot safer if we slept together tonight."

Saskia's breath caught in her throat. Trying to adopt the same careless tone he was using, she said, "I think that's a great idea. That way, if one of us has a bad dream, well, the other one will be right there to help."

"Right there," he murmured huskily, edging over and nipping her on the ear.

Her arms were halfway around his neck when a pair of bright headlights raked the driveway. A long, large car sloshed right past them, splashing mud and rain across their windows.

"Who could that be?" Saskia demanded, sitting up straighter. "Did you see the size of that car?"

"That," he said in a deadly voice, "was my mother."

"WHAT HAVE THESE PEOPLE done to the place?" asked Honoria Wynn. She crinkled her nose. "It's simply ghastly."

"*We* like it," Petunia and Primrose said in unison.

"Mother, why are you here?" Connor ushered her into the parlor, with Saskia trailing after. The aunts fluttered somewhere behind that, clucking over the chauffeur, who seemed unfazed.

"Thank goodness the power came back. We wouldn't want to have a guest in the dark, now would we?" Petunia said.

But Honoria Wynn paid her no attention. "Well, Connor, someone had to come and clean up this mess." Her eyebrows rose in exaggerated horror. "Do you know that Mimsy Burroughs got one of those distressing brochures? I saw her at the opera Tuesday night, and she was going on and on about how she intended to drop down and see what the fuss was all about. Can you imagine? Mimsy Burroughs, tattling to all of New York about how the Wynns have been shamed in their own home."

"It's not ours."

"What?" She slapped a heavily ringed hand over her heart. "Not ours?"

"What?" the three Trueloves chorused.

"It's complicated, but it turns out we don't own this house. They do."

"We don't?"

"We do?"

With a suitably dazed expression, Connor glanced back and forth between them. Most everyone there knew that he was lying, but it didn't seem to matter. All he said was "Yes."

"Well, we'll have to see about this," Mrs. Wynn huffed. "I'll be on the phone to my lawyers, first thing in the morning. I'm not surprised, Connor, not at all, that you've botched this." Glaring at the lot of them, she heaved herself to her tiny feet and announced, "They've ruined you!"

"Don't be ridiculous, Mother."

"They ruined Bunky, and now they're corrupting you," she declared. "No better than they should be. Trueloves! Hmph. Might as well call themselves Free-loves. None of them are married, and yet they still manage to have children, don't they?" She sent a scathing glance Saskia's way.

"My parents were married," she returned coolly. "Not that it's any of your business."

"That's enough." Connor set himself bodily between them, unwilling to see his mother and his... Well, whatever Saskia was, he wasn't going to let her get into a fistfight in Wynnwood's parlor. "Mother, apologize to Saskia."

"Connor, really!"

"It's okay," Saskia tried, but he wouldn't let her get a word in edgewise.

"And what sort of name is Saskia, I'd like to know?" Mrs. Wynn muttered.

"This from a woman who named her daughters Buffy and Kippy." His hand protectively on Saskia's shoulder, he said, "I think Saskia is a beautiful name. Did you know that was the name of Rembrandt's wife? And there happens to be a famous and very striking painting called 'Portrait of Saskia.'"

"I didn't know you knew that," Saskia murmured.

"There are a lot of things about me that you don't know."

"I'm beginning to figure that out."

But he would deal with that later. First things first. "Apologize, Mother." He lowered his brows. "Now."

"For what?" she inquired.

There was a pause. "Since you have insulted everyone here, and apologizing individually would take too long, a general apology will do."

"Hmph." She pouted, but she eventually gave in, waving the famous Wynn diamonds in the air. "All right then. So sorry."

"That's not good enough," he persisted, but all of the Trueloves descended on him at once.

"It's late, and she's tired," Aunt Petunia tried. "Don't fret, dear. She'll be herself in the morning."

That was exactly what he was afraid of.

Petunia added, "We've accepted her apology, haven't we, dears? So why don't we get Mrs. Wynn a nice cup of tea and a cookie, and then we'll tuck her into bed and everyone will feel ever so much better."

"You're staying here?" he asked his mother.

"Of course she's staying here!" Primrose exclaimed. "Why, we wouldn't have it any other way."

"I'll just run up and get a room ready," Saskia said in a rush.

He caught her by the hand. Bending down, he whispered, "But what about...?"

"What?"

"What we decided." His voice fell even lower. "Fending off ghosts. Together."

"We can't. Not now," she responded. "Connor! Not with your mother here!"

"You were ready to go for it with your aunts here."

"They're different. They pride themselves on being unorthodox. But your mother..."

"But her being here doesn't change the fact that we might be in danger from the ghost." He cast a baleful eye over at his mother's forbidding face. "Although she *is* pretty scary. You think she's scary enough to keep the Commodore away?"

"Connor! It will be all right. Listen. The rain has stopped." She offered an encouraging smile. "Everything will be fine now that the rain has stopped. No dreams in the rain, remember?"

"All right." He dropped a small kiss on her cheek, more for his mother's benefit than anything else. Too bad if the old snob didn't like it. "In the morning then, okay?"

"The morning."

And then she raced up the stairs to fix up a room, while his mother ordered the chauffeur to bring in her luggage and the whole household hopped to like a bunch of servants.

SHE COULD'VE BEEN sleeping with Connor tonight. He'd asked, hadn't he?

What a great idea...

Saskia groaned. What had she been thinking of? Kissing him in her dreams. Kissing him in the secret passage. Kissing him on the lawn of the Jekyll Island

Club. Almost kissing him in the front seat of a 1971 Volvo station wagon with bad tires.

It was as if the only time she could breathe was when her lips were attached to his.

"But, you know," she mused, "it would have been nice to be tucked in with Connor. Or at least to have him sleeping outside my door, so no goblins or spooks could come sailing in."

Instead, she was right next door to his imperious, demanding, bad-tempered mother. She cursed her luck again that the only room she could put old Honoria in was the one right next door to her own.

She tried to be quiet as she prepared for bed, not wanting to disturb the frightening Mrs. Wynn. Wincing, she eased open her creaky window, taking a deep breath of the heavy, humid air. The night seemed pregnant with the possibility of another thunderstorm, and she wasn't at all sure her fragile nerves could take it.

It was as if the skies mocked her, sending her exactly what she didn't want. She cringed as a fierce boom exploded outside somewhere, followed by a sizzling streak of lightning only seconds later. The storms were back.

As the heavens began to open up with hard, hot rain, Saskia closed her window. Her room was in the north wing, where the air-conditioning had been behaving before, but not tonight. The air felt very close and stuffy in here.

At some point, she didn't know when, her aunts must've infiltrated her room with their romance-inducing candles, since there were now two fat red candles that smelled of roses glowing on her dresser. The light was comforting in the dark, however, and she left the candles burning as she threw the covers back over the ornately carved foot of her antique bed and then tried to sleep in the sweltering room.

Her hair was sticking to her forehead, and she got up once to tie it back and splash cool water on her face. She got up again to check her vent, to make sure it was open all the way. She felt a trickle of cool air coming out, but it didn't seem to help.

Saskia tossed back and forth on the soggy sheets, wondering if she was awake because of the heat or just because she kept remembering what she could have been doing in that bed.

Lumping her pillow into a new shape, she turned over on her side, facing the candles, watching the tiny flames flicker hypnotically.

She lost track of time. She was so hot. So tired.

Her eyes fluttered closed and she smiled, thinking of Connor's face, his hands, that birthmark he had on his thigh.

Or was that the Commodore's birthmark? She kept meaning to ask him . . .

"Good evening, my love," he said evenly.

"Connor?" she mumbled sleepily. He seemed to be standing right next to her bed all of a sudden. Where did he come from? "I thought we agreed that while your mother was here, we'd try to be good."

"My mother?"

"You remember. She came tonight." She squinted at him. "What are you wearing? I've never seen you wear anything like that before?"

It was a dressing gown, probably silk, in a dark maroon-and-black paisley pattern. A bit longer than knee length, the robe was loosely belted. Very loosely. Most of Connor's smoothly muscled chest was visible in the deep vee at the neck, and a good deal of bare leg was showing as well.

"Connor! That thing is shameless. You didn't walk down the halls in that, did you? Where did you get that hideous robe?" She sat up in bed immediately wondering if she was having another dream, but he seemed too real. "It's not your style at all. You look like Hugh Hefner at the *Playboy* mansion."

He cocked his head to one side. "Whatever are you babbling about? You gave it to me for my birthday, silly goose."

"Silly goose? Silly goose?" But Connor didn't use phrases like that. Unless he was... "Oh, dear. You're not Connor, are you?"

But he acted as if he hadn't heard her at all. He frowned down at his robe. "I think it's rather handsome myself. One of my favorites."

"C-Commodore?" she inquired. "Is that you?"

"Of course, it's me." He arched an aristocratic eyebrow. "I hope no one else is in the habit of visiting your bedchamber at this time of night, darling."

"Oh, my God. What am I going to do?"

Was this really Connor, possessed by the ghost of the Commodore? Or maybe he was still sleeping in his own bed, and this was some sort of independent phantom. Could the Commodore choose how he wanted to materialize?

"Perhaps you've changed your mind and no longer fancy the dressing gown. Ah, well." He shrugged. Carelessly, he tossed the silk robe aside. "Is this more to your liking?"

Good God, he was naked! He'd dropped his robe as if it was no big deal and then just stood there, completely and unbelievably naked. Saskia gaped. Not only was he naked, but he was also completely aroused and completely gorgeous.

"Put that back on!" she managed to choke out. She snatched up the sheet and held it in front of her eyes like a Victorian virgin. Dreams were one thing. But she had just discovered that seeing him in the flesh was something altogether different. "Are you... Did you... Are you wearing it again?"

"I sometimes forget what an innocent you are, my sweet." His voice was silky, indulgent, when he said, "But we both know you have your moments that are anything but innocent, don't we?"

But at least he was partially clothed again.

She shook her head, trying to make heads or tails of this. She'd been visited by the Commodore in her dreams, and she'd been with Connor when he was visited in his. But this...

How was she supposed to handle a three-dimensional ghost, a naked ghost, from a different time, when he thought she was his mistress?

Saskia shook her head. It made no sense.

Meanwhile, instead of coherent thoughts, all she could get into her brain was the repeat image of Connor standing there without a stitch. If she'd thought

her temperature was as high as it could go before he
got there, she was certainly wrong on that count.

Good God in heaven, he had a beautiful body. Was
that really fair?

She took a surreptitious peek, looking for that little birthmark on his thigh, the one she'd noticed in her
first nocturnal fantasy. But she wasn't sure whether
that was Connor's birthmark or the Commodore's. Or
maybe they both had it. And if the Commodore was
walking around in Connor's body, and he had a
birthmark, then whose was it?

She was never at her best when she was tired, but
this was beyond disoriented, beyond confused. This
was incoherent.

In light of anything better to do, she took a defen-
sive posture, edging herself all the way up to the
headboard and clinging to its carved cupids for dear
life. How odd that she'd been willing to share a bed
with Connor, but she was petrified by his alter ego.

"Well, I don't know him as well," she muttered
under her breath. "*He's* not the one I'm in love with."

"What are you gibbering about, my sweet child?"
He bent closer, twining a short tendril of the loose hair
at her temple around his finger. "You'd better not be
in love with anyone but me."

His fingers brushed her cheek. She tried not to notice. How exhausting, how terminally irritating, to
suddenly realize that she was in love with him, only to
find he had turned into someone else before her very
eyes.

"Isabelle," he remarked sternly, "are you listening
to me?"

"Could you please keep your voice down? Your mother is right next door."

"My mother died fifteen years ago," he said flatly.

"No, not your mother. Connor's mother!"

"I don't care whose mother she is, my love." His lips hovered next to her ear, tickling her with the soft, hot puffs of his breath. "I only want you."

As he edged one strong knee onto the bed, she couldn't help looking down there, in between the silken folds of his dressing gown. "You're making what you want abundantly clear," she said hoarsely.

He smiled wickedly, catching her by the wrist, lowering his lips to kiss and then gently bite the soft, fleshy part of her hand. Saskia swallowed around a dry throat.

This strange incarnation of Connor whispered, "Would you like to see just how much I want you, darling? I am fully prepared to prove my case."

"I can imagine," she whispered.

As he advanced, she leaned back even farther on the bed, but there was nowhere to go. Her bed was built right into the room, an immovable object stuck up against two walls. It was a gorgeous thing, all wild and ornate, and the major reason she'd chosen this room as her own. But because of its configuration, she was pretty much trapped there in the corner, unable to get to the light switch or the door.

Connor—or the Commodore—bent down to relight the candle on her bedside table. As the wick sputtered into flame, Saskia noted uneasily that a small statue of some kind had been placed on the table next to the candles. She couldn't see it clearly, but she knew it hadn't been there when she'd last looked at that table.

"I do so like candlelight, don't you, my love? I like to see the expression on your face when I make love to you." He smiled. "You moan so very prettily."

The light played over his face, casting his chiseled features into deep shadow. But there was no mistaking the look in his eye. The hunter.

And she knew who his prey was.

He lay a hand under her chin, softly caressing the line of her jaw. He smiled. "My sweet, sweet love. We both know exactly what you want, don't we?"

He might be weird, but he still looked and felt like Connor, and she had very few defenses left when it came to him.

All she could get out was a breathless whisper. "Uh, what would that be?"

"Me." Negligently, he removed the sheet from her lifeless fingers. He covered her lips with his own and kissed her, heavy and deep and slow, sliding one hand to the back of her neck, the other to cup her breast. With the edge of his thumb, he barely teased her nipple through the thin fabric of her cotton nightgown.

Melting into him, she closed her eyes. She was tingling and trembling, incapable of resisting. It was all so slow, so languid, so lovely...

Until he murmured, "Isabelle, you enchant me."

"Isabelle?"

"Come here, darling," he ordered, yanking her down under him. "I've had enough of the coquette for one night."

But the fact that he'd called her the wrong name made it all seem terribly wrong. He might look like Connor and feel like Connor, but that wasn't enough.

"I can't make love with you," she whispered.

His hands slid up under her nightgown. "Oh, yes, you can."

Without thinking, she reached over onto the nightstand, got a good grip on the metal statuette sitting there, pulled back and bonked him one.

As he went out like a light, his body slumping half off the bed, she realized what she had done. "Oh, my God! I hope I didn't kill you. Connor? Connor, are you in there?"

Although he had a good-size bump, his pulse was strong and steady. "You'll be okay," she told him. "I'm really sorry, but Connor, he wasn't you. I just couldn't."

She stood back and surveyed the damage, the statue still gripped in her hand. For the first time, she took a good look at the weapon she'd grabbed up so hastily from her bedside table.

She gasped. "Holy smokes. It's me!"

It was small, no more than eight inches tall, with elegant curves and the hint of motion, as if the tiny, nude woman it depicted might spring to life at any moment.

Peering at it, holding it closer to the candlelight, Saskia suddenly felt very sure of what she saw. It was in the slight smile, the tilt of the head, the stubborn chin.

"It's me," she said faintly. "Me and Isabelle. This must be one of the Isabelle bronzes."

It was lovely. There was no question of that.

"But why," she brooded, "why does it have to be nude?"

She had never been all that crazy about her own body to start out with it, but it was wrenchingly embarrassing to see it immortalized in art. With a squeal of distress, she set it back on the table. Didn't she have a handkerchief or anything to drape over it?

"This is ridiculous, Saskia," she told herself. But she found a scarf in her drawer and dressed the thing, and she actually felt much better.

Except for Connor, of course.

"I'm sure you'll be fine," she informed his inert body.

But what was she going to do with him, now that he was a big unconscious lump half on and half off her bed? He was way too heavy to drag all the way back to his own room.

In the end, the only choice was to heave him all the way over onto the other side of her bed. But as he lay sprawled there, only partially covered by that indecent silk dressing gown, she just couldn't get in with him.

What if he woke up and was still the Commodore, still intent on this playboy seduction scene? That robe would afford no protection at all, for either of them.

So she sneaked down to his room, very quietly found a pair of pajama bottoms, and then tried to wrestle him into them on her bed. She had never thought much about how delicate an operation it might be to fit a nude, unconscious man into his pajamas, but she was rapidly finding out.

Feeling like a real ninny, swearing under her breath, she inched the pants on over his feet, tugged one pant leg up his calf, and politely averted her eyes when she got up to the knee.

But it was even stickier doing it by touch. And then there was the birthmark question.

She hesitated, his pajamas still around his knees, as she tried to decide just how rude she was willing to be.

"Oh, the hell with it."

Brazen and shameless, she yanked the edge of the robe aside and looked her fill. All sinew and muscle. All fabulous.

"Birthmark," she whispered. "Bingo."

It looked like a little butterfly, etched into his hip where it angled into his thigh. It was really kind of sweet. How many men had butterflies on their hip-bones?

She touched it with the tip of her finger, and sort of smiled at it.

"Ohh," he groaned in his sleep, and she snatched her finger back as if she'd been burned.

Too bad she couldn't tell from the sound of his groans whether he was still the Commodore or safely back as Connor.

Just to be on the safe side, she took the belt off his dressing gown and tied one of his hands to the bed-post. That would at least keep him under control if he woke up and was still inside some other persona.

If she'd needed proof that his theory was right, that he was good and truly possessed, he'd walked in the door with it tonight.

Connor looked so innocent lying there, breathing gently, his hand tied to the bedpost, nothing like a robber baron from another century. But how else to explain this?

"Poor Connor," Saskia murmured, leaning down to brush a kiss on his cheek. "You'd better come back to me, do you hear? In the morning, I want *you* back. Not him."

And if he wasn't himself in the morning?

She vowed, "I'll find a way to get you back, if I have to exorcise you myself."

Chapter Eleven

She awoke to the steady thump of his heartbeat, right under her ear.

"Good morning, beautiful," he mumbled drowsily, dropping a warm, soft kiss on the back of her neck. His arms tightened around her middle, pulling her back more securely into the seductive curve of his long, hard body. He fell back asleep with Saskia in his arms.

Saskia just lay there, her eyes wide open. At some point during the night, he'd lost the long silk robe, because she could feel very clearly that his chest and his arms were now bare. At some other point, he'd gotten his wrist out of its silken knots, because both of his arms were around her, and his hands were firmly attached to her body.

If she tilted up a little to one side, she could see the empty loop of silk, still hanging from the bedpost. Meanwhile, his left hand had cozied up to her rib cage, while his right hand pressed her firmly into his lap.

It was a very charming domestic scene, the sort one might imagine waking up to with a longtime lover. Unfortunately, she had no such longtime lover. But if things stayed this way much longer, she was going to get one very soon.

She bit her lip. It was very hard not to just shut her eyes and go back to sleep, and let him deal with it when he woke up.

On the other hand, her nightgown was already bunched around her thighs, and if the two of them got any more tangled up, she was going to wake up right in the middle of something she wouldn't be able to stop. And she wouldn't even be sure who she was doing it with.

That furnished a good enough reason to get out of there.

As carefully as possible, she eased out from under his arms, backing out over the side of the bed. She'd gotten both feet on the ground and she was just sliding her nightgown back down to where it belonged, when he raised his head and asked sleepily, "What are you doing?"

"Getting up?"

"Oh. Saskia?"

She sighed with relief. At least he knew who she was. That was a good sign that she wouldn't be fighting off the advances of that masher from the past, the Commodore. Just to be sure, she ventured, "Connor? Is that you?"

"Who else would it be?"

"You don't want to know."

At that, he blinked. He stared at her for a moment, and then blinked again. "What do you mean?"

"Let's just say you haven't been yourself recently."

His eyes opened wide, and he sat up abruptly, looking around the room in confusion. "What am I doing here? How did I get here? Where am I?"

"This is my room, and I don't know how you got here. Walked, I guess." His consternation would've been funny, if it weren't so embarrassing. She wished she knew how much he remembered. "You showed up in the middle of the night."

He shot a glance down at his lap. "Why are my pajamas on backward?"

"Backward? Are they?" She felt her face flame. Awkwardly, she said, "I was trying to hurry, and I didn't notice they had a back and a front."

"Huh?" He was wrinkling his forehead so tightly she thought he might faint from the exertion. "You mean you took off my clothes and put me in pajamas? Backward?"

"No," she protested, "I didn't take you out of anything. You weren't wearing any. Clothes, I mean."

His mouth fell open. "I was running around naked? When?"

Saskia knew she was going to have to be careful. The last time he'd emerged from a bout with the Commodore, he'd been horrified, shocked, embarrassed, ready to commit himself to a funny farm, or maybe just run away forever.

What would he do this time, when things had gotten so much trickier? Once he found out how naughty

the Commodore had been in his body, he was really
going to be steamed.

"How did I get here?" he demanded again, louder
this time. And then he yowled, "Ow, my head!" and
clamped a hand over the lump she'd made. Unfortunately for him, he picked the hand she'd tied to the
bedpost. "Ow! My wrist." He sent her a scathing
glance. "What did you do, beat me up before you stole
my pants?"

"I didn't steal your pants—I told you that! I put the
pants on, remember?"

"Backward," he growled.

"Right." She began to pace in front of the bed,
waving her arms as she raced through an explanation.
"Okay, look, there's no way I can sugarcoat this.
We're just going to have to deal with it, okay? So let
me just say that you came in here last night, very late.
You were wearing a slinky robe and nothing else, and
you tried to seduce me. In other words," she concluded, "you came in here as the Commodore."

His face was a study in horror. "Last night?"

"Yes. I'm really sorry, Connor." She crawled back
into the bed, close to his side. "But it isn't your fault.
We both know it isn't your fault. And we will find a
way out. In fact, I have a plan. I think we should have
a powwow, with my aunts and Madame Renata. They
may not be the best spiritualists around, but they are
close at hand. Maybe they can help us think of some
way to send the Commodore back where he came
from."

But Connor said nothing, just flopped back into the bedclothes with a black look on his face.

"This really upsets you, doesn't it?" she asked softly.

"More like it wounds me, down to my very soul. I have no control over it. None." He swore under his breath, and smacked a fist quietly into the sheets. "I can't stand the idea that he can come and go as he pleases, and I have nothing to say about it. This time, I don't even have any memory of it. Damn it, Saskia," he said through gritted teeth, "it's getting worse."

Concerned, she set a cool hand on his forehead. "Connor, are you okay?"

"Does it sound like I'm okay? I appear to be living a double life and trying to seduce people in my sleep, and you ask if I'm okay?"

"I meant physically," she said tightly, sitting back on her heels. "I thought I might have hit you too hard and you had a concussion or something."

"You hit me? My head is pounding like this because you *hit* me?"

She frowned. "Look, I'm sorry—okay? I wasn't trying to hurt you, just demobilize you for a while. What was I supposed to do? You were very insistent." Recalling her own conduct, she blushed again. She planned to leave the part about melting in the Commodore's arms right out of her narrative. "I had no choice but to knock you out. So I did."

"Good God."

"I know it's shocking, but Connor, listen, you have to get past that, because I think we should try to—"

"You *hit* me," he said again. "And what about my wrist?"

"Oh, that." She focused on the waistband of his pajama bottoms, where there was this intriguing whorl of copper-colored hair, just below his belly button. In a small voice, she said, "I tied you to the bedpost."

"You did *what?*"

"You heard me. I tied your hand to the bedpost! Right there. I don't know how you got it out, because I tied it really tight." He looked so scandalized, she offered an explanation without even being asked. "If you woke up and were still the Commodore, what was I going to do? I wanted to make sure I could control you."

He looked at the silk belt, still tied to the post, down at his wrist and then back at the belt. And then he dropped his head into his pillow. "Saskia, I am so sorry," he whispered. "I can't begin to explain. My conduct has been simply unthinkable. That you would find it necessary to knock me out and tie me to the bed . . . God, I am so sorry. I could've hurt you."

"But you didn't. Everything is fine." Lying down next to him, she offered him her best, brightest smile. "I'm just so glad you're back. I had a few bad moments there, when I wondered if he might be taking over for good."

"But he could've, don't you see?" He gripped her shoulders in his hands, trying to make her understand. "At any time, he can come flying back in, and there's not a damned thing I can do about it."

"Well, I can." She smiled. "I can hit you over the head again."

"How can you find this funny?"

"Because I realized something last night." She scrambled to look him right in the eye. "Whatever happens, I'm not giving up. However many times he takes over, I'll get you back. Because we're a team, remember? Whatever happens, we're in this together. And, Connor..." *Oh, brother.* But there was no easy way to do it. She took a deep breath, and then came right out with it. "When he came swaggering in here and thought I should fall into bed with him, I just couldn't. Because I knew then. He may look like you, but I don't love... him. I love... *you.*"

She might've hoped that he would be as thrilled with the news as she was. But he looked stricken. "How can you love someone who doesn't know who he is half the time?" Connor said, still reeling over her declaration of love.

"I don't think you get a choice in this sort of thing."

"Saskia, you cannot love me," he insisted, but knew that he didn't want to believe otherwise. He started to get out of bed, but fell back with a big "Ouch!"

Obviously, this was not the right time for declarations of love. Not with the headache he had.

"Look, there's something else you should know," she told him in order to change the subject. "Something I think you're really going to like."

Reaching over for the small statuette, discreetly wrapped in its improvised scarf sarong, she brought it back to brandish in front of him. "You dropped this off here last night. Somehow, wherever you were, you brought back a memento from Isabelle."

"The bronze," he whispered reverently, unwrapping it immediately, running his fingers over its tiny breasts and miniature hips. "It's priceless. It's beautiful. It's..." His gaze rose to meet hers. "It's you! And it's nude!" He made a funny noise deep in his throat. "Very nude."

"About as naked as you can get." Retrieving the discarded scarf, she hastily covered up that wanton little bronze body. "I don't know why Isabelle had to take off her clothes at the drop of a hat, if she was going to look just like me. It's embarrassing."

"Oh, come on. It's beautiful." With a smile, he stole it away, holding it out of Saskia's reach as he undressed it again. It gave her a very funny feeling in the pit of her stomach when he ran his fingers over that miniature version of her own body in such a proprietary way.

"It's embarrassing."

"If you think so, imagine how the Commodore felt," Connor said idly. He was tilting the statue, letting the morning light catch it in different ways, as if he were absolutely captivated by its impudent little charms. "Remember, somebody had to sculpt this. Which means another man—our friend, the bohemian, Gabriel Roques—was hanging around for long periods of time while the Commodore's girlfriend posed in the nude."

"You know, you're right. Isabelle already had a bad reputation, and this would've clinched it."

Connor shrugged. "I guess that's why he hid it away, so no one would ever see it but him. So where did this come from? I was stumbling around Wynnwood last night, dragging this along with me?"

"I guess so. All you had with you was that silk robe and the statue."

"Silk robe?"

"This thing," she said, bending down and scooping it off the floor. "It's the Commodore's, too, isn't it?"

"It's certainly not mine."

"This is great," Saskia said lightly. "When the Commodore visits you, he takes you places and gives you toys you don't remember afterward. All he does is try to seduce me."

Connor clenched his jaw. "I don't seem to have a choice as to what I do and don't do. And I have no recollection of last night, so I don't have any idea where the robe or the statue came from."

"Well, I'll tell you what." She slid out of bed, crossed to the window and threw it open wide. "Next time I see the Commodore, I'll ask him where he hides his stuff. Okay?"

"Don't you dare." Connor snatched up the paisley dressing gown and the bronze statuette, and strode purposefully for the door. His jaw was clenched tight and a pulse pounded in his temple, not far from where she'd hit him. She winced, sorry all over again. Tersely, he said, "I'm going to get some aspirin for

this headache you gave me, and then I'm going to see
if I left any clues last night—like maybe a secret door
standing open somewhere.''

"Connor, you can't," she hissed, throwing herself
in between him and the door. "Your mother might be
out there."

"All right, all right. So you'll have to go get me
some clothes. We'll get rid of my mother somehow,
and then we'll hold this powwow you want. But in the
meantime," he ordered quite fiercely, "I don't want
you anywhere near the Commodore."

"Connor," she called after him, *"you're* the Commodore!"

"CONNOR," SASKIA SAID under her breath, "how did
she get here?"

The portrait of Isabelle was now cozied right up
next to the fireplace in the parlor.

"My aunts and your mother were playing gin
rummy in this very parlor, not five minutes ago," she
swore. "You came and got your mother to take a
phone call from Puffy—"

"It's Buffy."

"I know. Anyway, you came and got your mother,
and my aunts absconded with their winnings. I gave
them a lecture about fleecing guests, I came back, and
now Isabelle is sitting over by the Commodore." She
stared at the painting. "You didn't bring her down
here from the secret room, did you?"

"Of course not. I haven't been back up there."
Considering that neither of them knew where he'd

wandered while under the Commodore's influence last night, he added, "At least not as far as I know."

She moved a little closer, taking his arm for security, and they both gazed, awestruck, at the mysteriously mobile painting. "Do you think *he* brought it down here?" she whispered.

"We know he can move things when he wants to. Remember the books in the library."

"Oooh, that's creepy. Can you imagine coming down for a cool drink in the middle of the night and watching an oil painting fly by over your head?"

Connor brushed his thumb over the small brass plate. *Isabelle, 1904.* "He's getting bolder," he said grimly. "This is a more obvious move."

"Who's getting bolder?" somebody stage-whispered right at Saskia's elbow, and she jumped about a foot in the air.

Hand at her heart, she mumbled, "You scared me, Aunt Primrose."

"The Commodore, hmm? Is he moving things around the house? That's very common with ghosts, you know." Primrose nodded sagely. "Madame Renata told me so."

"Yes, indeed!" the medium announced in her deepest, most dramatic voice as she, too, swept into the parlor. She was decked out in full regalia today, with the sparkly gauze caftan and the bejeweled turban. "I do indeed feel the presence of a poltergeist!"

"Join the club," Saskia muttered. She still thought the medium was about as psychic as a slab of cement, but there was no arguing with her results. Not with the Commodore going bump in the night.

"I understand you have need of my services," Renata said, flourishing one long trailing sleeve. She almost knocked a deck of cards and a pad of paper off the card table, but it didn't stop her. "I shall put all of my considerable spiritual resources at your command to exorcise this tormented spirit, to send him packing back to the Great Beyond, to darken your door no more!"

It was stylish, but hardly necessary.

"Oh, dear, no!" Primrose hurried to tell her. "We mustn't exorcise him. Not yet. I'm sure he must have come back because he had some task that needed completion, some deed that must be done. It would be simply awful to send the poor man back without getting his mission squared away."

"I think you're mixing this up with that TV show," Saskia put in kindly. "The one where the guy travels through time righting wrongs—"

"Oh, no, I'm not." Primrose set her thin lips in a stubborn line. "Why would he come back and haunt us, unless there was something he had to fix?" She crossed her arms over the front of her apron. "It only makes sense."

"I think she's right," Connor told them. "He wants something done, and it has to do with Isabelle. The visions, the painting, the statue—it all adds up to Isabelle."

Petunia came running in all aflutter. "I must have missed something," she said eagerly, pulling at Connor's sleeve. "I don't know about any of those things. Visions, paintings, statues?"

"Have you been holding back, Saskia?" Primrose inquired sourly.

It took some time to go over all the paranormal phenomena the Truelove sisters and Madame Renata had missed out on. By the end of Connor's story, with many additions and corrections from Saskia, they were all sitting around the table jostling to be heard, and Madame Renata was so excited she was scribbling notes under the gin-rummy scores.

"This hardly seems fair," complained Primrose. "We're the witches, and they're having all the fun!"

"Would you like us to try a few potions?" Petunia asked helpfully. "I'm sure we could mix up something." She gave Saskia a big, fat wink. "Because you know, we've been doing so well with our potions lately."

"No potions," Connor said flatly.

"The key here is that we'd like this stuff to stop," Saskia intervened. "We'd like to stay away from potions, but if anyone has any other ideas—"

"I vote with Primrose." Petunia raised her small, plump hand. "We have to right the wrong. Only then will the Commodore's spirit rest in peace."

"But what wrong?" Connor was a study in impatience. "We've already been through this. The only thing we can think of is that all those busybodies in 1904 thought Isabelle was a scarlet woman." They had all begun to speak of Isabelle and the Commodore in the most normal fashion, as if they lived down the street. "And it hardly matters if we spruce up her reputation after all this time."

"We don't even know how their story ended," Saskia noted. "He tried to introduce her to society as his fiancée—that's what Connor saw at the Jekyll Island Club—but that didn't work. We presume they were still together for at least a little while after that, because he came prowling to my room looking for her."

Petunia's eyes lit up. "You didn't tell us that part, dear. What happened?"

"Nothing," Connor and Saskia said in unison.

"Well, it can't have been a happy end." Primrose, always ready to see the dark without the dawn, added her contribution. "He married Connor's great-grandmother, and they had a family. There's no room for Isabelle there, I'm afraid."

"So maybe we're supposed to find them a happy ending at last!" Petunia cried, clapping her hands together.

"It's not possible." They hadn't heard much out of Madame Renata, but she drew herself to her full height and stared them all down. "We must exorcise the Commodore. It is the only way."

Petunia's face crumpled. "No sort of cosmic wedding ceremony you could perform, I suppose, uniting them in celestial matrimony forever after?"

"Hmph," the medium snorted. "No, I feel the Commodore is a tormented soul who will never be happy. Let's banish him."

"Absolutely not!" Aunt Primrose shouted. "Why, that's barbaric."

As the three older ladies thrashed it out, Saskia quietly asked Connor, "What do you think?"

"I'm ready to try anything.

"Research!" trumpeted Primrose. "We'll find out everything we can about Isabelle. If we know what happened, we can help the Commodore find peace."

"Exorcism!" Renata shot back. "We'll have a blowout of a séance, and send him packing."

"Now, now, ladies." Aunt Petunia tapped a finger against her pert mouth. "We could do both."

Both heads swung around.

"Well," Petunia continued, "I think we should have a séance, just as Madame Renata suggests. We'll see if we can't call him up and ask him what the trouble is. If we can fix it, so much the better. But if we can't, we'll blast him," she said cheerfully.

"I like it!" the other two cried.

Saskia and Connor shared doubtful glances.

"Do you have a better idea?" he asked her.

"Not really."

"What have we got to lose?"

"Exactly."

And so, with great trepidation, they all sat down together and drew up their plans.

"Tonight, if we can manage it," the aunts concluded. "Tomorrow, at the latest."

"Well, all right, but—"

"No buts." Petunia had begun to act more like a drill sergeant than her usual sweet, hopeless self.

"Renata will round up all the psychic heavy hitters she knows between Jacksonville and Savannah to help get the spiritual energy flowing. Primrose and I will do preliminary research, to see where Isabelle went off to. We'll see if there's anything at that little library in the basement of the club. If not, we'll get Higgins to drive us to Brunswick."

"Higgins?" Saskia asked, mystified.

"Mother's chauffeur," Connor told her.

Petunia nodded vigorously. "Such a sweet man. We're now the best of friends." She went back to her list, checking off items with a slash of her pencil. "Saskia will be in charge of getting things ready for all the guests who'll be arriving for the séance. Food, drink, and whatever you'll need to get rooms in order for about ten psychic professionals."

"Ten?" Saskia repeated. "But, Aunt Petunia, I'm not sure we can afford that."

Connor whispered. "Don't worry. I'll foot the bill for this one. I'm the one in dire need of exorcising."

"Okay. If you're sure." But she was feeling very apprehensive, nonetheless. What if something went wrong and they brought the Commodore back full force, and then couldn't get rid of him? What if they were visited by a whole host of unhappy spirits, each one worse than the last?

"And what about me?" he asked. "You've given everyone a job but me."

"Your mission is to keep your mother occupied," Petunia said firmly.

"Now, wait—"

"She's a lovely woman, but a tad headstrong. She's already informed us that she doesn't believe in ghosts, that she won't allow séances at Wynnwood, and then..." Aunt Petunia dropped her voice. "She accused us of cheating at cards."

"But, darling, you do cheat at cards," Saskia reminded her.

"Never!" the sisters said with spirit.

"Surely you can find something better for me to do than—"

"But that's just it." Her eyes wide and sincere, Petunia patted Connor on the hand. "This is a very important task. And besides, dear, you're more centrally involved in this than the rest of us, due to the Commodore's fondness for using your body. It might be nice if you tried to rest and relax before the big event."

"You want me to relax and escort my mother at the same time? Not possible."

"It's not a bad idea, Connor," Saskia ventured. "I don't get to do anything all that crucial, either. And you might enjoy it. It's a beautiful day—not a cloud in the sky," she said meaningfully.

"But what am I going to do with her?"

"Bicycle around the island?"

He just snorted.

"Miniature golf? Croquet on the lawn of the club? Shopping on St. Simon's Island?"

"Shopping," he groaned. "I'm going to die."

"No, you're not," Saskia said severely. "That's the whole idea."

HER ARMS FULL OF bedspreads and grocery bags, Saskia came running back to Wynnwood. There was tons to do before people began arriving, but she was dying to find out how the others had done with their assignments.

But neither her aunts nor Madame Renata were anywhere to be found.

"Hello?" she called out. With a feeling of foreboding, Saskia did a quick search of the places they usually hung out. But no Petunia, no Primrose, no Renata.

And then she realized she hadn't seen Connor, either. He was probably still off shopping with his mother, but she had visions of him staked out somewhere, while her aunts rubbed him with magic ointments and amulets, trying to bewitch the demons out of him.

"Connor," she called out. "Where are you?"

But of course he didn't answer. They probably had him bound and gagged. She raced up the stairs in search of him.

Premonitions of disaster gripped her. She stood stock-still at the bottom of the main stairs, holding onto the newel post for dear life, trying to come up with new theories as to where they might be.

As she stood there, she realized the one place she hadn't looked. The garden. It was a nice day, after all, and maybe Connor had taken his mother for a stroll there.

Smiling with relief, Saskia hightailed it out the back door. But instead of Connor she found Primrose, half up a tree as she stuffed leaves in a little pouch. "Get down from there," Saskia said sternly. "What are you doing, Aunt Primrose? What are those leaves for?"

"I need leaves with just the right spots of powdery mildew," Primrose explained patiently. "See this one? Perfect."

"Charming. And aren't you supposed to be diligently researching what happened to Isabelle?"

"Oh, well, we found that in five minutes."

"You did? Well? What happened?"

Petunia popped up on the other side of the tree, quickly enough to startle Saskia. Petunia smiled her most mischievous grin and wiggled a finger back and forth at Saskia. "Patience, my dear."

"Please, Aunt Petunia. What did you find out?"

"She died."

"She died?"

"Well, of course she died." Petunia gave a little shrug. "We were very lucky, actually. Higgins drove us to the library, and it seems he knows all about running microfilm machines. And so we found an obituary, quick as you please. She died right here at Wynnwood in 1904. But that was all there was about her."

"Here, in 1904? But that's the date on the painting. She was very young, then." Saskia was suddenly swamped with sadness. Softly, she asked, "How did she die?"

"Well, we don't know. It didn't say."

"But why didn't you find out?"

"Look here, Saskia," Primrose started, dangling dangerously from the tree. "We did the best we could. That's all there was. We'll find out the rest at the séance tonight. The important thing is that she was the love of the Commodore's life, and she died. And that is most certainly the wrong we need to right."

Saskia was so anxious to hear the details that she felt like hopping up and down until they told her. "So the séance is set for tonight? Did Madame Renata find enough people?"

"Oh, she did just fine. Three psychics, a past-life regressionist, two channelers and another trance medium." Petunia's eyes sparkled with excitement. "Seven. Plus us, that's twelve all together, which Renata thinks is just right. Our guests should start arriving any time."

"But where is Madame Renata? I didn't see her in the house."

Primrose swung down out of the tree. "Oh, she and Mrs. Wynn are out here, too. They're cutting white roses and wisteria to set in the parlor to cleanse it of alien elements, while Petunia and I try to put together the ingredients for a stabilizing tonic. Look, here come Renata and Honoria now! Isn't the wisteria lovely?"

"Don't tell me you've got Connor's mother embroiled in this, too?" Saskia began, but she was interrupted by a strange crunching noise, and then a loud masculine moan, both coming from the direction of the formal rose garden, where an arbor and several gravel paths were laid out in a perfect circle around...

"The birdbath!" Primrose announced.

As Petunia murmured something like, "Oh, my," Madame Renata added, in that thunderous voice of hers, "It's the Truelove curse!"

"Their family has a curse?" Mrs. Wynn demanded. "What is wrong with these people?"

Saskia took off at once, arriving in time to find Connor sprawled over a rosebush. "Are you all right?" she asked, patting him down for broken bones as she helped him pry his clothes off the thorny bush.

But he swatted her hands away. "I'm fine."

"What happened? What are you doing in the rosebush?"

"Somebody pushed me."

"Pushed you? Why would anyone do that?"

"I don't know." He grimaced, pulled a nasty thorn out of one hand, and then swiped angrily at the blood. "I almost fell right into the birdb—" He broke off abruptly.

"The birdbath? Where Bunky Wynn died?" Saskia felt all the color drain from her face. "It is the Truelove curse."

Connor tried to reassure her, but she wasn't having any of it. "First you're possessed, and then I'm cursed!" she cried. "You know, I really didn't need this as an added complication. But it's my own fault. I should never have told you I loved you," she said in a rush.

But by then the others had caught up with them, and they were all clamoring to speak.

"You told him you loved him?" Connor's mother bellowed. "Why, the very idea! I simply won't hear of it."

"It's the curse," Primrose wailed. "I knew we should have hung amulets on her bed."

Saskia did her best to tune them all out, as she knelt at his side. With his face cradled in her hands, she promised, "Once this is all over I'll give you up, if that's what it takes to stop the curse. But first, Connor, first we're going to get through this séance, and we're going to keep you safe."

"I'll be fine," he whispered. "Don't worry."

"Séance?" Mrs. Wynn shrieked. "She's going to put you through a séance?"

And then she fainted dead away, becoming the second member of the Wynn family within the space of ten minutes to narrowly miss hitting that blasted birdbath.

Chapter Twelve

Connor fidgeted, tapping two fingers on the tablecloth. From all the way down at the other end of the long oval table Saskia sent him an encouraging smile, but he could tell she was every bit as agitated as he was.

She looked lovely in some kind of creamy white dress, but her smile kept wavering and there was a decided light of panic in her eyes.

He didn't blame her. He had never been crazy about the idea of séances at Wynnwood, and he still wasn't. Especially with this band of crazies and lunatics, assembled for the express purpose of conjuring up a ghost he had never wanted to meet in the first place.

And they really were a flaky bunch. He used to think the Trueloves were weird, but next to these characters, they seemed like the Brady Bunch. Even Renata paled by comparison.

The first psychic to arrive was a man dressed in a shiny green suit, with oily jet black hair combed down *over* his eyes. How did he see? Second sight, apparently. He called himself simply Calamari.

At first Connor thought the name was a joke. Who would want to call himself *Squid?* But Calamari seemed to take himself very seriously. He took one look at Connor and shuddered, refusing to shake his hand.

The next arrivals were a shapely young woman stuffed inside a skintight purple-velour catsuit and thigh-high leather boots and the seven-foot-tall Russian channeler who came with her. He was wearing a cape like Count Dracula.

Oddest of all was the lone past-life regressionist. Her name was Helen, and she had thick glasses and a head cold. She looked like a stereotypical small-town librarian.

No, he decided, oddest of all was his mother, Honoria Wynn, the fashionable society matron who didn't believe in ghosts, but who'd insisted on taking part in the event.

Renata had pitched a fit, claiming that Mrs. Wynn brought their numbers to thirteen and threatened disaster, but Connor's mother was very good at pitching fits of her own and she got to stay. He didn't know how many of the whys and wherefores she'd figured out, but he didn't plan to tell her, that was for sure.

Right now, she sat there demurely in her Chanel suit, trying very hard not to get within six inches of anybody who was suspect—which in this crowd was everyone.

As per Madame Renata's instructions, Connor sat between the medium herself and Aunt Petunia, with his back to the fireplace. Renata was very clear that this was the optimal spot for him, but Saskia had to sit way down at the end, between the cat lady and the squid man.

Connor let out a long breath, trying to remain calm. Although he couldn't see his great-grandfather's face in the portrait from where he sat, it felt as if the Commodore's eyes were boring a hole in his back.

They were all ordered to sit in a specific order, with their chairs exactly positioned, just so many inches apart. Renata really got into this positioning stuff. It took several minutes before she was satisfied that they were all sitting properly, with just the right number of candles, with the flowers positioned the way she wanted.

God, he was nervous. He wished Renata would just get this thing going, but she was going back over all the seating arrangements, redoing one candelabra and then another. Clearly, she was enjoying getting to be the big shot in front of all her paranormal friends, and she was going to take her moment in the spotlight.

Finally, when everything appeared to be set to her satisfaction, as they all peered through the dim candlelight, she pulled her big wing chair up to her place, grandly poured herself a glass of red wine from a cut-glass decanter that had been set at her place and took a long swallow. Then she slapped her hands down, palms up, on the leather arms of her chair, tossed her head back into her chair and began to snort and mumble to herself.

A murmur went up around the table among the other spiritualists, who were apparently contemptuous of her opening rigmarole. "I've seen better at the circus," the cat lady sniffed.

"Silence!" Madame Renata boomed, raising her head and glowering down the table. She wasn't putting up with professional rivalries here. "I am absorbing the psychic vibrations."

"Yeah, right," her adversary muttered.

Renata gave her a look that made it clear she wouldn't be invited back for more fun society parties if she didn't clam up. "If everyone is quite ready," she intoned. "The spirits await us, and we must begin."

She pointed a long finger at each of them in turn. "The spirits require our concentration and our deepest thoughts. We must focus all our energy, my friends, as we search through the stars, through this world and into the next. It is a difficult and perilous journey we undertake. Are you committed, mind and body, to help us?"

She waited, boring her eyes into them, as each person in the circle nodded quickly. When she got to Connor, he pressed his lips into a stubborn line. Committed, mind and body? They all ought to be committed, all right.

But in the end, he nodded, too, trying to open his mind to whatever was going to happen. He wanted the Commodore gone for good, didn't he? If this was the only way to do it, so be it.

"You must all remain perfectly silent and still while I enter my trance state. Once my spirit guide has arrived, he may pose questions to better direct our inquiry. Do not be afraid. He is a gentle spirit. You may answer him, but do not shout or scream, simply answer as calmly as you can manage."

She certainly had a whole routine going here, didn't she? Connor glanced around to see if anyone else was feeling as much like a stooge as he was, but most of them were sitting there like good little psychic soldiers, eyes closed, in various states of concentration. Next to Connor's mother, Count Dracula was humming tunelessly, and his huge head bobbed and weaved in rhythm.

"I am ready to begin. Hands, please." The medium grabbed for Connor's hand on her right and Primrose's on her left, as the rest of them linked up around the table. She had a grip like a stevedore, and Connor winced in pain as she crushed his fingers. On the other side, Petunia's tiny, plump hand was warm and shaky, as if she was filled with too much energy and excitement to hold still.

Count Dracula reached for Connor's mother, who shrieked "Do I have to?" in a disgusted tone that made it sound as if she'd been asked to eat worms. The others shushed her quickly, until she shut up and took the count's massive hand.

"Concentrate," Renata commanded, in that deep, resonant voice of hers. "Concentrate. Tonight we seek the spirit of Commodore Edmund Wynn. His image is above the mantel before you. Focus on that image.

Etch it in your mind. You may look as long as you like, but when you have a firm and resolute fix on his image, please close your eyes to lock it in. Think of nothing else but the Commodore. Keep that image constant.''

He couldn't see the painting from where he sat, but he really didn't need to. He knew the Commodore's face: it was his own.

Under the table, he felt something slide past his leg with a swish and a spark of electricity. He had a moment of panic, until he heard a soft meow and realized it was just Banquo, who had the uncanny knack of popping up whenever his presence added atmosphere.

For the time being, Connor decided to keep his eyes open. He pretended to concentrate on the Commodore for about thirty seconds, but it just wasn't the sort of thing he had a lot of patience for. He tried, but there was just no way.

Next to him, Madame Renata appeared to be dozing. Slumped in her wing chair, she had her eyes closed, with her chin tucked into her chest. She was mumbling something, the same few syllables over and over again, but nothing he recognized as a word. But she still had that iron grip on his hand.

The seconds dragged into minutes and nobody moved, nobody spoke. The cat came back and rubbed itself on Connor's leg for a while, finally settling down and going to sleep on his foot. He could hear someone else at the table breathing rhythmically, as if he or she had fallen asleep, too. Probably that slinky cat woman.

"I call upon you, Mike," Renata said suddenly, in a chesty, rumbling voice that shocked everyone at the table back to life. "Mike, come to me! Come to me, now!"

Mike? He thought they were supposed to be going for the Commodore.

"Her spirit guide," Petunia whispered.

Connor didn't know what a spirit guide was, so he kept his mouth shut, watching Madame Renata contort her face into grotesque expressions and make funny noises under her breath. This was what they'd all been running around like crazy trying to set up? As if this nonsense could conjure up more than a few dust motes.

"Mike, is that you?" the medium cried out, and then she answered herself, whispering, "Yes, Renata, I have arrived to guide you," in a high-pitched, tinny voice that sounded so ridiculous he couldn't believe any of the others were buying this.

Connor peered at Saskia through the dim light. He hoped she was all right down there, with her hand squashed inside the oily fist of that squid man. But it was too dark to tell.

"I have journeyed a long way to come to you to-night," Renata cried, in that same thin, quavery voice. Her head dropped back even farther, and she rocked it from side to side, in time with her words. "Through wind and rain and storm, through many lives and many ages."

Connor got the distinct impression that this was a well-rehearsed performance, that she used the same exact shtick every time she got her paws on a new batch of suckers. He began to feel very annoyed that he'd let himself in for this silliness, or that he'd ever thought for one moment this would accomplish anything.

"I feel the spirits all around me," "Mike" continued. "They are very agitated here in this place. This is a place of old unhappiness, of lives entwined and knotted, souls still seeking earthly peace and celestial reward. Many voices. Commodore Wynn, where are you? It is your voice we seek to hear. Tell us why you still roam the halls of Wynnwood. Tell us, Commodore, tell us what you want from us."

There was no answer, at least not from the direction of Renata or "Mike." But suddenly, without warning, there was a scream from the foot of the table and the sound of a chair crashing to the ground.

Was it his mother? Had the seven-foot Russian made a pass at her under the table?

"What is she doing?" Honoria Wynn asked loudly. "Why is she getting up? No one gave us permission to get up."

It was Saskia. Connor's heart leapt into his throat. She stumbled away from the overturned chair, her eyes wide, her hands outstretched in front of her. He made a move to go to her, but Renata grabbed him by the arm with one big hand.

"No," she said fiercely. "She's in a trance! The spirit must have come through her instead of me. But you mustn't touch her—especially you. It could jerk her out of the trance too quickly, or send her in even deeper. You stay over here, as far away as possible.''

This was out of his league. He stilled, unwilling to risk hurting Saskia.

Silently, Saskia edged farther away from the table, past the cat lady and the squid man, who both scrambled to get out of her way. Back she went, skirting a couch and a love seat, staring at everything as if she were trying to get her bearings.

At his side, Petunia cried out, ''Saskia, dear, what is it?''

But she didn't answer, just kept moving around in that weird, skittish fashion, gazing at all of them, seeing no one.

''What's wrong with her?'' the tour-guide wife demanded.

''She's in a trance state, and very unstable from the looks of it,'' Renata announced. ''This isn't good. An amateur in so deep— I just don't know.''

''But what do we do?'' Primrose asked anxiously. ''Saskia, dear, answer us, please!''

Racking his brain for some way to be of help, Connor slammed over to the wall to turn on the lights. Saskia blinked a few times, but didn't seem any more lucid. He could see that her pupils were dilated to the size of dimes, and her eyes looked huge and dark, troubled.

It was as if she were crying out soundlessly for him to help her and he didn't know how. He had never felt more inadequate in his entire life. His hands curled into fists, and he smashed them into his pockets.

The others seemed to be more interested than concerned. "Could it be the Commodore?" the Calamari man murmured. "Yet it seems strange that with all of us here to choose from, a spirit would go for *her.*"

Petunia called out, "Commodore, is that you?"

But Saskia ignored her.

"The last time we asked for Poppy, but we got the Commodore instead," Primrose said logically. "You don't suppose this time we asked for the Commodore and got Poppy?"

"Poppy?" Petunia cried, waving her arms at Saskia. But no reaction greeted her. "Pansy?" she tried, obviously grasping at straws. "Mother? Father? Bunky?"

Suddenly it hit Connor. How stupid could they all be? It was staring them right in the face, after all. "Isabelle," he said loudly. "Of course, she's Isabelle."

Saskia turned and looked right at him. "Darling?" she asked. "Who are all these people?"

And then all hell broke loose. A cold wind seemed to whip up from out of nowhere, slashing at their clothes, toppling incense burners, tossing lamps off tables, scattering Madame Renata's white roses like grains of sand. It roared around them, ferocious and savage, as the flames on the candles grew higher and higher.

But where was that gale coming from? There were no windows, no doors open in this parlor. How did gusts of wind spontaneously generate like that?

Connor stood rooted to his spot. Saskia gazed at him, mysterious and beautiful, as the impossible wind dashed the full skirt of her white dress around her legs and whipped her hair around her face.

Luminous with love and hope, as if the bizarre wind and rain couldn't touch her, she sent him a glowing smile, holding out her arms to him. "Darling," she said, "I knew you'd forgive me. I knew it. Come to me, my love."

He didn't care what Renata said; he couldn't refuse her. He strode to her side, plucking her up into his arms, pressing her close. "Of course I forgive you," he whispered. "Always."

"Always," she said with a sigh. And then her body went limp in his embrace.

"Saskia?" As he tipped her back against his shoulder, her mouth fell open slightly, but no words came out, just a soft "Ohh..." Connor stared, paralyzed with fear, as her eyes rolled back in her head. Saskia was out cold.

"Saskia?" he tried, frantic to revive her. But she just lay there in his arms, as cold and perfect as the bronze statue in her image.

"I warned you not to touch her," Renata said spitefully.

"Be quiet!" Aunt Petunia shot back. "He did the only thing he could've done."

Hoisting Saskia's slender body up into his arms to carry her, he said tersely, "I'm taking her upstairs. You get rid of all these people. And then we're going to do our best to figure out how to help her. Do you hear me?"

"Of course, dear," Petunia assured him.

And then he swept out of the room, cradling Saskia in his arms.

"STILL NOTHING?" Aunt Primrose ventured.

They were all hovering around Saskia's bed, with Primrose carrying cold compresses and smelling salts, and Petunia toting a prayer wheel and a handful of little colored stones she called *chakras*. They had all agreed that a doctor wouldn't help, because there was nothing physically wrong with her. Although he hadn't said anything to her aunts, Connor had decided he would only wait until morning.

If there was no change in her condition, he would personally fly her off the island to see a brain surgeon, a psychiatrist or a witch doctor—or perhaps all three. Whatever it took.

Whatever happens, whatever we need to do to sort this thing out, we're in this together. Her words echoed in his brain. She had been so strong, so sure. Why couldn't he?

The first moment I saw you, there was already this connection built into my heart . . .

"My heart, too," he whispered. "I should have told you."

Gently, he tucked a stray tendril of hair back from her face. Her eyelashes lay dark against her pale cheek. "She looks very peaceful, doesn't she? Like she's sleeping."

"She *is* sleeping," Petunia put in. "Just having a little nap. And when she wakes up, I know she'll be herself again."

"But we don't know that at all." He knew it wasn't her aunts' fault. If anyone's, it was his. She had been searching to find answers for him, grasping at straws and séances, so worried that something might happen to him, and yet *she* was the one who'd ended up in danger. Angrily, he said, "This isn't fair. It should've been me."

"Oh, dear," Primrose murmured in her most quavery voice. "She will be all right, won't she?"

Petunia reached out and hugged her sister. "Of course, she will."

As Primrose burst into tears, Connor ran a shaky hand through his hair. He had no idea what to say to comfort them, any more than he knew what to do to bring Saskia back to life.

"Look," he began, with a firm hand on each aunt, "I know that you love her, and that you want to help. But would you mind leaving me alone with her for a little while? I think that would be best."

"Are you sure?" asked Petunia, lifting her prayer wheel hopefully.

"I'm sure."

But when they were gone, the silence in the room was deafening.

"Saskia, what am I going to do?" he asked quietly, lifting her limp hand to his cheek, brushing it back and forth. Her skin was so cold. "I thought the séance might be dangerous, but to me, not you. I never thought anything would happen to you."

The very idea that he might never see Saskia again was like a knife twisting in his gut. *When she wakes up, she'll be Saskia again,* he told himself. *I always woke up from the Commodore.*

But how did he know this was the same? And what if it wasn't?

Crawling into her bed, he carefully slid her up against his chest. "Saskia," he said softly, "please come back to me. It's important, because I didn't get the chance to tell you. You told me that you loved me, and I was too wound up in getting rid of the Commodore to realize what a gift that was."

He had never spoken like this to anyone. A major declaration was hovering on his lips. If only the one person in the world he wanted to hear it would wake up and listen.

"I love you," he whispered, holding her close to his heart. "I love the way you look at me and the way you always hold your chin up, like you expect somebody to take a punch at you. You're funny and smart and loyal, and you don't take anything from anybody. Please, Saskia," he begged her, "please come back to me so that I can tell you all the things I should've said before."

His heart leapt. He thought he saw her eyelids flutter. But as he kept up his vigil, there was no more movement.

Saskia dreamed on.

SHE SIGHED. He was furious with her. And she was so very tired of fighting the same fight again and again.

Her teacup rattled against the saucer as she set it down. Feeling very gloomy, Isabelle gazed out the window, watching a bird flit from one gnarled branch to another on the big live oak tree.

She wished she were a bird. She wished she could fly away into freedom, across the blue, blue ocean. And never be shouted at again.

"You are deliberately trying to provoke me," he argued. "You could fit into society if you wanted to, but you prefer to be an outcast, to mock all of us. I had almost repaired the damage you did the last time, and now I find myself embroiled in yet another scandal."

"I like to enjoy myself, that's all," she said darkly. "Unlike the rest of you."

"And enjoying yourself—does that include staying out all night, drinking wine in disreputable cafés with disreputable Frenchmen?" He was so angry a vein pulsed in his temple.

"I was in France, my love. Who else was I to drink with?"

"No one, preferably."

"But, darling," she protested, "I was on holiday. I was having fun. How was I to know that that odious

Mrs. Whatsit-Whoozit would decide that she simply must see the Moulin Rouge, and walk into the very café where I was arguing politics with a coterie of Marxists. It was frightfully stimulating.''

"I can well imagine."

"Oh, Edmund, really. I have told you time and again that I am not the right sort of woman for you." She heaved a larger sigh. "Why does that fact continue to surprise you?"

"But you are the woman for me. The only one," he said passionately, kneeling in front of her, gazing up into her enchanting face.

"I love you, darling, with all my heart." *But I love my freedom more.* Why was she so torn—torn between this deep and abiding hunger for the likes of upright Edmund Wynn on one hand, and a desperate need to be free on the other? Perhaps it was because she had never brought herself to believe that he loved her, all of her, completely and absolutely, and not just the portions that fit into his tidy, little world.

"But what do we really have?" he asked gloomily. "You won't appear in public with me. You won't fight for me."

"We have our island," she said softly.

"But there is a world out there, Isabelle. And if you would just take my arm and stare the gossip down, we could let them all know that we are together and we don't give a damn what they think."

"Ah, but that is exactly the problem, my love." She pulled his head into her lap, gently stroking his hair. "You do care what they think, and you always will."

"I don't—" he insisted.

"Shh. Let's talk of something else, shall we?" If she didn't relieve the awful tension compressing her heart, she knew she would explode. In a suitably lively tone, she announced, "I met the most entertaining man when I was in Paris. His name is Gabriel Roques."

"The artist?"

"Then you've heard of him?"

"He's been in New York of late. Painting extremely flattering portraits of all the most fashionable women."

"He's a bit full of himself, I'm afraid, quite the egoiste, but supremely talented. Edmund, I'm so very flattered, because he says he wants to paint my portrait. And then do a series of statues. Of me! Can you imagine?"

"I think you will be the loveliest subject he's ever had."

She laughed gaily. "I was hoping you'd say that, darling, because you see, I'll need you to pay for them. Mr. Roques is frightfully expensive."

"I think that can be arranged."

"You spoil me, my love."

"Yes," he said dryly, "I know. May I come and watch you when you pose, then?"

"Oh, no." She felt the first frisson of nervousness. The portrait was one thing; a host of very respectable matrons had posed for Roques portraits.

But a series of nude statues would be quite another.

But, damnation, the man was a genius! If he felt that her body could be immortalized, how could she decline. Oh, she was well aware that the Commodore would be very angry if he knew how she intended to pose. Not proper. Immodest. Yet another scandal at her door.

But once the statues were done and he saw how beautiful they were, surely his stifling sense of morality could be overcome. She could cajole him into anything, after all. She always had.

But her smile was a tad nervous when she said, "You must wait until we're finished. But the wait will be worthwhile. Mr. Roques thinks that my statues will be famous. Desired by every collector around the world."

"They will be unavailable to all his collectors. I will keep them, every one, close to my heart."

"Will you?"

"Yes." His voice was soft and seductive as he rose and held out his hand to her. "I've had cook make us a special supper tonight, to bring up to our tower room. Would you like that?"

"I would adore it." But as she took his arm, she whispered, "Edmund, whatever happens, will you promise that we will love each other always?"

He brought her hand to his lips. "Always."

Chapter Thirteen

Saskia awoke in the warm glow of sweet dreams. The room was dark and she knew it was still very late, but she had been jolted awake by a very vivid feeling.

He loves me! she thought, but she didn't recall hearing the words. Nonetheless, her heart felt quite sure.

"Connor?" she murmured. "Did you tell me that you loved me?"

"Hmm?" He lifted his head. She could see by the cloudy confusion in his eyes that he was not really awake. "Love you. Yes." He smiled drowsily and pulled her closer, covering her lips with his, kissing her deep and sweet. "Oh, yes."

And then he shot up in the bed.

"Saskia, is that you?" He wedged her head between his hands, scrutinizing her this way and that. "Did you come back?"

"Where have I been?"

"It was that absurd séance," he told her, kissing her quickly, hugging her, and then kissing her again.

"They were trying to get the Commodore, remember? But Isabelle apparently came instead." He paused. "I can't believe I'm saying this. But it doesn't matter. Because you're back. Thank God, you're back."

"Connor, I have no idea what you're talking about, but do you realize you're sleeping in your clothes?" Startled, she surveyed his button-down shirt and khaki trousers, and then her own wrinkled white dress. It had three little buttons on the bodice, and one of them was undone. What was going on here? "And this is *my* room," she realized. "Connor, your mother. She's right next door!"

"I don't give a damn about my mother."

"But I don't want her to think—"

He put a finger over her lips. "I don't care what she thinks. Saskia, I love you. That's the only important thing."

But his mother... She didn't know what to say. "Do you really mean that?"

"Absolutely," he whispered fervently.

"But we're so different from each other. And there are so many obstacles."

"Why are you raising this now? I don't care about any of that."

"But in my dream," she persisted, "Isabelle was so unhappy. She loved the Commodore, but she felt so constrained, so hemmed in, by everything he stood for. I think that's it, don't you, what they were trying to tell us?"

"You had another dream? And I didn't?"

"Yes, but forget that for a second." Beginning to feel that she was really onto something here, she took him by the arms and rushed on. "They loved each other, but they couldn't change their basic natures. He was so proper and so prominent, just like you. And she was a free spirit. The bronzes," she gasped. "She was just about to pose for the bronzes. That must have been the last straw."

"Saskia, you've lost me."

But she didn't have time to paint pretty word pictures. This was important. "Connor, do you think we're doomed, like they were? Because your mother hates me and I would never fit into your world, just like Isabelle?"

"Don't be absurd. We are not doomed," he said firmly. "For one thing, my mother hates everyone. And this is not 1904. If I marry someone who's a little unorthodox, it only makes me more interesting. All it will do is get me in the newspapers for a couple of days, and Wynn Industries will jump fifty points on the stock market."

But she was stuck back a few lines. "Marry? Did you say marry?"

"Of course." He kissed her hungrily. "We're a team, remember? Whatever happens, we're in it together. And that's what *I* think this is all about. The Commodore couldn't marry the woman he loved. But I can. So maybe he and Isabelle thought we needed a little unearthly push in the right direction."

Saskia slid her hands around the back of his neck, pulling him down to her. "Could you kiss me again, please?" she asked huskily. "And tell me again?"

"That I love you? Absolutely." He punctuated his words with quick kisses, on her lips and her chin, her cheeks and her nose, anywhere he could reach. "A million times. I don't really understand why it was necessary that you have that last dream and scare me to death, but I'm not going to ask questions. I just plan to enjoy the moment. God, do I love you."

"Tell me again."

"I would be happy to, except..." He paused, and the expression in his eyes took on a new spark of heat. "Except it's really hard to keep talking when you look at me like that. I don't want to talk."

She slipped one hand inside his rumpled shirt and wiggled her fingers against his smooth, warm skin. "There are times when actions definitely speak louder than words."

"Oh, Saskia..." But he caught her hand and held it, gazing down into her eyes. "Are you sure? You fainted, you know. If there's anything wrong, and we should take it easy, it's okay. I can wait."

"I don't want to wait. We've waited long enough."

"A lifetime," he said softly. "Two lifetimes."

She knew he must be at the end of his rope, exhausted from the emotional roller coaster of the past twenty-four hours. There were dark circles under his eyes and stress lines etched around his narrow mouth. She wanted to smooth it all away.

Since yesterday, he had not been himself, she had not been herself, she had feared for his life, he had feared for her life...

But through all of the storms, one thing remained constant. No matter where they were, no matter who they were, they still loved each other.

And as he pressed his lips to the pulse in her neck, as she melted underneath him, she knew in her heart that this was the absolute right thing to do.

Nevertheless, her hands were shaking as she fiddled with the buttons on his shirt. She was too eager, too impatient.

"What's the rush?" he whispered, as he nibbled her earlobe and breathed on her cheek.

But her heart pounded, and the blood seemed to roar in her ears. Her mind was a jumble of images of Connor and her, all wrapped together in passion and desire.

"All I've thought about, since the first moment I saw you, was getting you out of your clothes and making love to you." She shoved his shirt off his shoulders. "I want you. I want you now. If you make this take forever, I'm going to die."

He shrugged away the shirt, but then he caught both her hands in one of his own. "You're not going to die." His lips curved in a wicked smile. "And I am going to make it take forever."

"I may have something to say about that."

But he kissed her, long and sweet. "You talk too much, Saskia," he said darkly.

Clasping her hands over her head, he held himself above her in the bed, barely out of reach, lowering only his head as he fastened his mouth over hers. It had never been hard for Connor to stoke her fires, not hard at all. In fact, he seemed to have a real talent for it.

Every time he looked at her with those crystal blue eyes, she started throbbing and quivering from her head down to her toes.

"I want to touch you," she murmured, but he shook his head no, keeping a firm grip on her wrists as he brushed his lips over her neck and the line of her jaw.

It was bliss. It was torture. She loved every relentless, painstaking, interminable second of it.

Connor's mouth moved down farther, to the three small rosettes that held her bodice together. With his teeth, he twisted one loop out from around its button. It took forever that way, but the sight of his dark head pressed against her white dress and the feel of his teeth and his mouth just barely grazing her hot, moist skin was intoxicating. Slowly, so slowly, he undid the last rosette, loosening her dress enough to almost completely bare her breasts.

"Take it off, please," she said restlessly, moaning as she tried to arch her body higher, closer, more fully into his mouth. His lips and his tongue traced a line down the exposed edges of her dress, and her nipples grew taut and hard.

She ached for him to touch her, taste her. But still he resisted giving her what she wanted, only taunting, never sating.

Finally, he released her arms and slipped the dress off over her shoulders, letting the creamy fabric pool at her waist. Now his hands cupped her breasts more fully, and his clever, sinful mouth caressed and teased her, tugging her breasts into sharp peaks. She moaned with pleasure.

Dazzled with desire, she rubbed herself sinuously against him, shamelessly trying to push harder into the waves of sensation rocking her deep inside. He was smiling, damn him, while she was writhing and whimpering and completely losing control.

"This isn't fair," she whispered.

"Who said I was fair?"

And then he slipped a hand up under the full skirt of her dress, tracing a path of sparks up her calf, her thigh, her hip. His thumb skimmed the edge of her panties, tickling her, edging closer and closer. His fingers barely grazed her, not giving her nearly enough, just driving her insane with need and slick, hot desire.

"Oh, Connor, please..."

"I wanted this to last forever," he said, his voice no more than a raspy whisper, "but I find I just can't wait."

"If you wait any longer, I'll kill you," she returned.

His lips found hers as he stripped away her dress and her panties, and she scrambled to push away his pants, too, until it was just the two of them, skin to skin.

He held her for a long moment, brushing away her hair, watching her as if he wanted to memorize every detail of her face. He looked so mesmerized, so tender, that she fell in love with him all over again.

"I love you," she whispered. "Always."

Holding her close, Connor slipped inside.

Saskia welcomed him, matching him stroke for stroke, loving the feel of him, so much a part of her.

And then, just as she surprised herself by toppling over the pinnacle, she felt his whole, beautiful body going rigid under her hands.

"Saskia, I love you," he whispered hoarsely, as he lost himself inside her.

For a moment they just lay there, still entwined, listening as each other's heartbeats returned to a less erratic rhythm.

"Oh, my. Oh, my," she said languorously. She felt utterly and completely spent. All she could manage, as she snuggled closer, relaxing, unwinding inside, was a contented sigh.

Neither of them was wearing a thing, and their bodies were both slick with sweat and love, but they didn't care, just tangled together even closer, sinking deeper into the intoxicating feeling of finally being completely alone, completely together.

It was as if Morpheus himself had danced into the room, sprinkling magic dust on their eyes. Saskia yawned, sleepier than she'd ever felt in her entire life.

Her eyelids were so heavy, her body so warm and soft...

As their heads tipped together, they fell into deep, sweet, heavy sleep.

And then they began to dream.

ISABELLE WAS COLD. Cold and bored.

And she didn't like the look in the shifty eyes of Mr. Gabriel Roques. There was no question that he was a talented artist, a veritable genius with his hands, and the first few statues he had done were simply magnificent. But the longer she posed for him, the more Isabelle came to despise his generally unsavory attitude.

He glided over closer, intent on rearranging the sheer drape of white chiffon that slipped over her shoulder *à la grecque,* barely covering one of her breasts.

"I will adjust it myself," she said sharply.

"Lie still," he ordered, frowning as he fiddled with the fabric, moving it just so, edging it back to flow perfectly down the line of her body. "You've just tensed your muscles and completely ruined the arch of your back."

"I am not a statue, Mr. Roques, much as you enjoy thinking so."

He paid no attention to her complaint, just went back to his sketches and his models. "The last study had its charms, of course," he remarked thoughtfully. "A certain decadent quality perhaps, and a sharp political statement on the bourgeois stain of wealth. Nothing but you and your pearls." He grinned, and she felt herself stiffening with distaste. His mocking smile told her that the statue had nothing to do with politics and everything to do with erotica. "But I think this one, so provocatively undraped, will prove to be even more charming."

She was clinging stubbornly to the notion that she would be rid of the man very soon, and then she would be left with ten perfect little statues, all very artistic and lovely. No one—least of all Edmund—would ever know how humiliating her grand scheme to be immortalized had become. In the beginning she had been flattered and intrigued, and posing for Gabriel Roques had sounded like an amusing adventure. Instead, it was a dead bore. And a dangerous one at that.

"Could you please shut that?" she asked, shivering in the chilly April breeze coming from the large window behind him.

His eyes were heavy lidded as he stared at her. "But I like the texture of your skin better when it's cooler in here. You become waxy when it is too warm."

Delightful. He was lecherous *and* insulting. "Couldn't we move the studio somewhere else?" she asked plaintively. "I am aware that you like the light here, but we do run the risk that my friend, Mr. Wynn, will disturb us."

"Ah, yes, your friend the philistine. I'm sorry, lovely Isabelle, but we've started here, and we will finish here." He shrugged carelessly. "Once I find a studio that suits me, I am loath to leave. In any event, we seem quite secure here, all tucked away at the top of a tower. Perhaps that adds to my creative atmosphere.''

The words had no sooner left his mouth than Isabelle thought she heard the sound of a step on the circular stair. ''It can't be,'' she muttered. Edmund was hard at work at the club, sending telegrams back and forth to New York on some urgent business matter.

''Isabelle? Love, are you up here?'' a deep, masculine voice called. ''Darling, I have wonderful news.''

But as the door burst open, Edmund's wide smile descended into a look of absolute horror. His eyes raked her, and she was stunned into immobility.

''What is this?'' he gasped. ''What have you done?''

She clasped the chiffon to her breast, but it provided little cover. ''It—it isn't what you think, Edmund. It is nothing at all. Nothing. I am merely posing, for Mr. Roques's statue. I am garbed as Aphrodite, goddess of love.''

''But you are not garbed at all,'' he cried. And then he seemed to notice Gabriel Roques for the first time. ''Get out of here,'' he raged, lifting the man with one hand and shoving him at the stairs out of the secret room. ''Leave us, do you hear?''

''My hands... Don't hurt my hands,'' the artist begged, but he scurried out the door and down the stairs without a backward glance.

''Isabelle, how could you?'' Edmund demanded. His face was hard and cold. ''Do you think so little of me, of yourself, that you would degrade us both this way?''

"And what is degrading about posing for an artist?" Chin high, Isabelle tried to defend herself. "You said yourself that every society matron in New York has been painted by Mr. Roques."

"Not in the nude!" he shouted. "Only a harlot would drape herself in that disgusting manner in front of a man who is not her husband."

"A harlot? You forget yourself. You are not my husband." Rigid with anger, stung by his words, she crossed within inches of him, desperate to find something to cover herself. Edmund kept a few odds and ends up here, so that he had a change of clothes when they dallied in the secret room below. Moving to his armoire next to the window, she pulled open the doors, snatching out a dressing gown and wrapping it around her. "How dare you speak to me this way?"

"How dare I?" He grabbed for her wrist. "How dare you? Don't you know what kind of laughingstock I'll be once those statues you're so proud of blaze your shame in front of my friends?"

She tried to wrench her arm away. "What your friends think is once again your only concern. How telling, Edmund."

"Isabelle, this time you have gone too far."

"And what exactly does that mean? Shall you strike me next?" she taunted. They both knew very well that he would never raise a hand to her.

"You disgust me," he said coldly, and then he cast her away from him.

But she stumbled, and then her foot slipped on a carelessly flung length of silk. She saw that his eyes were wide with disbelief, but she kept falling, and the distance between them seemed to grow ever wider.

"No," he cried. "No!"

But it was too late. As he reached for her, Isabelle tumbled out the open window.

"NO!" CONNOR CAME AWAKE with a jerk, panting, sweating, scared. "No!"

Saskia sat up beside him.

"Oh God, did you have the same nightmare I did?" he mumbled, trying to breathe deeply, to get his erratic heartbeat to calm down. "Lord, that was awful. She went out the window, right in front of me. And I couldn't catch her." He squeezed his eyes shut, as if that would take away the terrible picture. "Oh, God. I still can't believe it."

But Saskia didn't respond.

"Saskia? Did you see it, too?"

Without a word, she scooted over to one side of the bed, grabbed hold of a flat wooden cherub worked into the headboard, and turned it sharply to one side. And then, before he had a chance to react, she jumped off the bed, picked up her robe and walked straight into her armoire.

How could she walk through an armoire?

"Another door into the secret passage," he said grimly.

In a flash, Connor was up and off the bed, shrugging into his pants, tearing after her. But all he saw was an armoire, half-full of Saskia's clothes. He tapped the back and the sides with the flat of his hand, but it sounded solid. Somehow, however, Saskia had flipped a switch and escaped. And then she'd apparently closed the door behind her.

"The cupid! There was a cupid on the bed, and she turned it."

It took only a second to go back to the headboard and spin the cupid, to try the armoire again. This time he saw that the whole back of the wardrobe had disappeared, an a yawning passage beckoned beyond.

He ducked through, half in and half out of the armoire. "Saskia," he called out, but his voice echoed in an empty corridor. Feeling very uneasy, he tried, "Isabelle?"

No answer to that, either. But he didn't have to reach her with his voice. He had no doubt where she'd run off to.

To the studio at the top of the circular stairs. The one in the dream.

Wedging the back of the armoire open with one of her sneakers, he grabbed a candle and some matches from her bedside table, and then he went after her.

It was even darker in the tunnel than it had been the first time, no doubt because he was making this trip in the dead of night. He lit his candle, which was better than nothing, but the light flickered unevenly on the narrowing walls, illuminating only a foot or two ahead of him as he climbed higher and higher in the house.

When he finally got to the top, to the place where the narrow staircase spiraled up into nowhere, he could see a square of light. A doorway. A doorway where there had been no door before.

His heart pounding in his chest, Connor flew up the curvy stairs, taking two at a time. As he raced into the room, the first thing he saw was the window on the far side, the big plate of glass that reached almost to the floor, that had made the room so attractive as a studio.

Right now, moonlight streamed through, creating the glow he'd seen from the bottom of the stairs. And lace curtains danced in front of it, catching the soft breeze.

But if there was a breeze, then that meant... The window was open.

His blood burned with adrenaline and fear as he raced to the window to look down. Panicking completely, he had to force himself to open his eyes and actually look.

Nothing. "Not there," he moaned. He sagged against the window, pressing his forehead to the cool glass on the top pane.

And then she touched him.

He spun around, pulse skyrocketing once more. But it was Saskia, the real one, the one with fire in her eyes. She must have been standing in the shadows, and he'd missed her in his single-minded dash to get to the window.

"Connor," she said, and he heard the anger and the tears in her voice. "Did you see it? She died, Connor. She died. He pushed her and she died."

"I know." First, he carefully backed up and slammed the window closed. No more accidents there. Ever. And then he pulled her into his arms, trying to offer what comfort he could. "But, darling, it was an accident. He didn't mean to. He never would've hurt her."

"It was still his fault. He said that she disgusted him!" Saskia pounded him on the shoulder. "And if he hadn't pushed her—"

"It was an accident," he said again. "He loved her."

"But how awful that she died that way. In the middle of a terrible argument, with everything so ... unfinished. It's so senseless."

"They would've worked it out, if only they'd had the chance. I know they would. They always had before."

"She died, Connor," she said dully. "And he died, too, didn't he? Inside."

"Yes, I think so," he whispered, remembering the anguish, the pain that had torn through him as he'd watched Isabelle fall away, just out of reach. He couldn't bear it.

"I think the worst part," Saskia said softly, "is that we didn't change anything. I mean, we know what happened now, and I suppose that's enough. But I really wanted to be able to change things for them." With a sigh, she gave him a wan smile. "They are beautiful though, aren't they?"

"They?" He turned. "Who?"

She blinked, incredulous, as if she thought he already knew. "The bronzes. The Isabelle bronzes."

There were about ten of them, clumped in a circle near the door. How could he have missed them? He must've come close to tripping over them on his way in. He bent, choosing the nearest one. If possible, it was even more beautiful than the one that had shown up in Saskia's bedroom. Where that one had looked like a woman about to burst into motion, this one was serenity, repose. Isabelle reclined against a pillar of some sort, with her eyes gazing into the distance.

"Beautiful," he said reverently, tracing a finger over her tiny bronzed face. "That's exactly how you looked when you told me that you loved you."

After a pause, Saskia commented, "Well, I think I had a few more clothes on."

"Forget about the clothes." He snatched up another then, and then another. "Each one is better than the last one. I can't believe it!" Like a kid in a candy story, he wanted to look at all of them at once. Out loud, he mused, "I was thinking that they should go to the Wynn wing of the Metropolitan, but then I thought, no, they deserve a special gallery of their own. Do you have any idea what a splash these beauties are going to make?"

"Are you serious?" She grabbed one away, an impudent, saucy one, with a laughing face. "But you can't put these on display. They look like *me!*"

"It will be hard to part with them. But you know, I can visit them as often as I like. And I admit, it's going to be a little strange to think of so many other men looking at my wife naked. But they're just statues, they're not you. And damn it, these deserve to be seen." He cradled the one he had chosen as his favorite, the soft, reflective one. "They truly are extraordinary." He laughed out loud, pulling Saskia into his embrace, in the middle of all those statues, kissing her on the tip of the nose. "You're beautiful, and they're beautiful. Extraordinary!"

"How very strange," she whispered.

Surprised, he looked down at her. "What is it? Why are you trembling?"

"Didn't you feel it?" She shivered, hitching her robe closer, snuggling into him, smiling mysteriously. "When I first came up here, all I could feel was this tension, this anger in the room. But then, I don't know, just a second ago, it was like a cloud of good feelings just swept right through the room. It felt like..." Saskia's smile widened. "Peace."

Epilogue

"How wonderful," Petunia said happily. "Our dearest hopes realized! Connor and Saskia have found each other, the restless spirits have found peace, and we get to stay at Wynnwood where we belong. Isn't it exciting?"

"Well, I'm not sure everything is settled," drawled Honoria Wynn. She happened to be wearing one of her more unpleasant faces. "We're going to have to pull down all the wallpaper and dispose of every rug in the house, if I'm to make this place look like a proper Wynn residence."

"We're giving you carte blanche on the decorating. Go hog wild," Saskia told her mother-in-law-to-be cheerfully. She tried to pretend she didn't notice Mrs. Wynn's sniff on the word "hog." Oh, well. What was life without a few wrinkles?

Linking her arm around Connor's neck, she let him pull her down next to him on the window seat. From where they sat, she could see the whole line of those elegant bronzes, arrayed on the library table to catch the sun until they could find a more suitable place for them. She smiled. "Aren't they just the prettiest things?"

He murmured, "No, you are, but they're a close second."

"Oh, those two," Aunt Primrose complained as she set down the tea tray and a plate of cookies. "Always necking and such. How are we to make plans?"

"You're perfectly capable of handling the séances all by yourselves," Saskia told her. "I cook, Saskia faxes back and forth to tell the fat cats in New York what to do and Mrs. Wynn decorates. And you guys take the spiritual connection. After all, you're a lot more paranormal than Madame Renata and her cronies."

And she added silently, *And a lot less likely to cook up a real ghost.*

"What a compliment!" Petunia chirped. "We shall not fail you, dear Saskia. Of that you can be sure!"

"But there is one thing, dear," Primrose put in, using her usual quavery voice of doom. "What about the Truelove curse? After all, Connor did get pushed in the garden. And neither the Commodore nor Isabelle strikes me as the sort to go pushing people into rosebushes."

"Oh, no." Saskia sank even farther into the chair. "I'd completely forgotten about that. Really, Connor, the Trueloves do have a terrible track record."

"I don't mind being the first man to catch and keep a Truelove. Besides," he told her with a definite cynical edge, "I plan to be very careful."

"But what about—"

"Hush," he said calmly. "If there are a few unexplained phantoms and wraiths still hanging around Wynnwood, knocking people over in the garden, then that will leave something for your ghost-busting guests to find, won't it?" His eyes were very blue, and very amorous, as he began to nuzzle Saskia's neck.

"Primrose, Honoria," Petunia said very suddenly. "I think there's something we need to attend to in the kitchen."

"I dislike kitchens," Connor's mother said with a wave of one hand.

Primrose looked blank. "What's in the kitchen?"

"Something. Now," persisted Petunia, dragging the other two women out the door in a hurry.

"I'll say one thing for Petunia," Connor murmured, just before he bit down gently on Saskia's earlobe.

Her head drifted back onto his shoulder; she was melting quickly. "Hmm. What's that?"

"She knows when to make an exit."

"Mmm, hmm. Must be her supernatural powers."

He scooted her around to face him, pulling her legs up onto the window seat. As he lazily lowered his lips to hers, she smiled and closed her eyes. But before his mouth got there he suddenly sat up very straight, almost dropping her off the window seat.

"Saskia, did you see that?"

She followed the line of his gaze, well out into the garden. "Where?"

"There—by the wisteria arbor. It's the damnedest thing."

"Isabelle," she said, her eyes round and surprised. "Isabelle and the Commodore."

There they were, big as life, strolling along in the garden. Isabelle was wearing a white lace dress and she was carrying a parasol, spinning it gaily as she walked. Edmund looked tall and handsome at her side, every bit as charming as Connor, and he bent down, eager to catch every word from the woman he loved.

Arm in arm, laughing and chatting, they ambled on, losing a bit of clarity now, and then a bit more. Their images grew fainter and fainter, until they had completely faded away, leaving behind no more than a pleasant glow near the wisteria.

"I guess this means they're happy," Saskia whispered. "And wherever they are, they'll be together."

Behind her, Connor wrapped her in his arms. "Together," he said. "Always."

HARLEQUIN®

AMERICAN ◆ ROMANCE®

You asked for it...and now you've got it. More MEN!

MORE THAN MEN

We're thrilled to bring you another special edition of the popular
MORE THAN MEN series.

Like those who have come before him, Sean Seaward is more than tall,
dark and handsome. All of these men have extraordinary powers that
make them "more than men." But whether they are able to grant you
three wishes or to live forever, make no mistake—their greatest,
most extraordinary power is that of seduction.

So make a date next month with Sean Seaward in
#538 **KISSED BY THE SEA**
by Rebecca Flanders

MILLION DOLLAR SWEEPSTAKES (III)

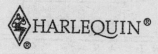

HARLEQUIN®

Weddings, Inc.

WEDDING INVITATION
Marisa Carroll

Brent Powell is marrying Jacqui Bertrand, and the whole town of Eternity is in on the plans. This is to be the first wedding orchestrated by the newly formed community co-op, Weddings, Inc., and no detail is being overlooked.

Except perhaps a couple of trivialities. The bride is no longer speaking to the groom, his mother is less than thrilled with her, and her kids want nothing to do with *him*.

WEDDING INVITATION, available in June from Superromance, is the first book in Harlequin's exciting new cross-line series, **WEDDINGS, INC.** Be sure to look for the second book, **EXPECTATIONS,** by Shannon Waverly (Harlequin Romance #3319), coming in July.

American Romance is goin' to the chapel...with three soon–to–be–wed couples. Only thing is, saying "I do" is the farthest thing from their minds!

You're cordially invited to join us for three months of veils and vows. Don't miss any of the nuptials in

GTC

**This June, Harlequin invites
you to a wedding of**

Celebrate the joy and romance of weddings past with
PROMISED BRIDES—a collection of original historical short
stories, written by three best-selling historical authors:

> *The Wedding of the Century*—MARY JO PUTNEY
> *Jesse's Wife*—KRISTIN JAMES
> *The Handfast*—JULIE TETEL

Three unforgettable heroines, three award-winning authors!
PROMISED BRIDES is available in June wherever Harlequin
Books are sold.

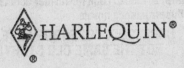

PB94

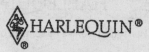

HARLEQUIN®

Don't miss these Harlequin favorites by some of our most distinguished authors!
And now, you can receive a discount by ordering two or more titles!

HT #25551	THE OTHER WOMAN by Candace Schuler	$2.99	☐
HT #25539	FOOLS RUSH IN by Vicki Lewis Thompson	$2.99	☐
HP #11550	THE GOLDEN GREEK by Sally Wentworth	$2.89	☐
HP #11603	PAST ALL REASON by Kay Thorpe	$2.99	☐
HR #03228	MEANT FOR EACH OTHER by Rebecca Winters	$2.89	☐
HR #03268	THE BAD PENNY by Susan Fox	$2.99	☐
HS #70532	TOUCH THE DAWN by Karen Young	$3.39	☐
HS #70540	FOR THE LOVE OF IVY by Barbara Kaye	$3.39	☐
HI #22177	MINDGAME by Laura Pender	$2.79	☐
HI #22214	TO DIE FOR by M.J. Rodgers	$2.89	☐
HAR #16421	HAPPY NEW YEAR, DARLING by Margaret St. George	$3.29	☐
HAR #16507	THE UNEXPECTED GROOM by Muriel Jensen	$3.50	☐
HH #28774	SPINDRIFT by Miranda Jarrett	$3.99	☐
HH #28782	SWEET SENSATIONS by Julie Tetel	$3.99	☐

Harlequin Promotional Titles

#83259	UNTAMED MAVERICK HEARTS (Short-story collection featuring Heather Graham Pozzessere, Patricia Potter, Joan Johnston)	$4.99	☐

(limited quantities available on certain titles)

	AMOUNT	$
DEDUCT:	10% DISCOUNT FOR 2+ BOOKS	$
	POSTAGE & HANDLING	$
	($1.00 for one book, 50¢ for each additional)	
	APPLICABLE TAXES*	$ _____
	TOTAL PAYABLE	$ _____
	(check or money order—please do not send cash)	

To order, complete this form and send it, along with a check or money order for the total above, payable to Harlequin Books, to: **In the U.S.:** 3010 Walden Avenue, P.O. Box 9047, Buffalo, NY 14269-9047; **In Canada:** P.O. Box 613, Fort Erie, Ontario, L2A 5X3.

Name: _____

Address: _____ City: _____

State/Prov.: _____ Zip/Postal Code: _____

*New York residents remit applicable sales taxes.
Canadian residents remit applicable GST and provincial taxes.

HBACK-AJ